" . . . t half a brain," Garner said quietly, "you'll go h . . . now."

H . . . e twisted. "Huh? What the heck are you talki . . . oss?"

" . . . gular idiot's errand, boy," Garner said. "If that . . . ch's isn't dead already, she's on her way to Braz . . . r someplace. And us going down to Galgo, tryin . . . er, is going to be the end of all of us."

" . . . how the heck you figure that?"

" . . . er been to Galgo, have you, Hobie?"

"Course not. You know I never been to Mexico."

"It's a tough town. As tough as they come. This auction has been going on for years, except nobody seems to know just where it's held, or leastwise, admits to knowing. Good men have tried and ended up murdered for their trouble."

"But Boss . . ." Hobie broke in.

Garner held up a hand. "Sam Teach is too close to the thing to see straight. He's going to do something stupid, sooner if not later, that's going to send us all home to Jesus . . ."

Titles by Wolf MacKenna

DUST RIDERS

GUNNING FOR REGRET

THE BURNING TRAIL

THE HELLRAISERS

THE
HELLRAISERS

WOLF MACKENNA

B
BERKLEY BOOKS, NEW YORK

THE HELLRAISERS

A Berkley Book / published by arrangement with the author

PRINTING HISTORY
Berkley edition / November 2003

ISBN: 0-425-18990-2

BERKLEY®
Berkley Books are published by The Berkley Publishing Group, a division of Penguin Group (USA) Inc., 375 Hudson Street, New York, New York 10014. BERKLEY and the "B" design are trademarks belonging to Penguin Group (USA) Inc.

PRINTED IN THE UNITED STATES OF AMERICA

10 9 8 7 6 5 4 3 2 1

1

Sam Teach had been down in Mexico, delivering a red and white Hereford bull to the rancho of Señor Carlos Ruiz Lopez. He'd raised the bull from a calf, and the animal was a fine one, strong and prepotent, and siring get that, even when he was bred to weedy, slab-sided longhorn cows, were stocky and round-muscled and fat. Señor Lopez had paid Teach well for him.

Teach felt bad about selling the bull. Mary had named him Teddy, and he'd eat from your hand and follow you around the barnyard like a dog, if given a chance. Teach felt so badly that he'd had to drown his sorrows in a great deal of port and sangria—at Señor Lopez's fine hacienda—and again later at the town cantina, in *cerveza* and mescal. But he comforted himself with the knowledge that when he got back home, the money from the bull would buy enough cows to more than double the size of their meager herd. Besides, he and Mary still had Turnip, Teddy's brother. He'd miss Teddy, though.

Once his hangover had lifted and he started on the long and dusty trail home, Teach thought about his Mary, and about the sweet roundness that, after years of hoping and praying, was at long last beginning to swell her belly. A son, he hoped. Well, a daughter would be fine, too. He'd been worried about leaving her.

"Go, Sam!" Mary had laughed, then pushed playfully at his chest. "For heaven's sake, I'll be fine! Pedro and Rance are here to protect me. Though from what, I haven't the slightest idea. There haven't been any Apache around here in years. Geronimo got carted off to Florida, in case you weren't paying attention," she teased.

He knew. He'd been in the cavalry then, and he'd help to load Geronimo on the train and send him into exile, along with his handful of braves, and along with the Apache scouts that had helped the Army to track him. Poor bastards. They'd sent them, enemies chained to enemies, to the Southern swamps in cattle cars.

He didn't reenlist when his time was up. He'd seen too much. He just wanted to take Mary to wife and build a house on that land they'd been scrimping for.

The house had been newly built, and Mary had put in a truck patch and a flower garden. To make it more homey, she'd said. They'd purchased a few cows, and he'd gotten a good deal on two yearling Hereford bull calves from a man named Jenkins, who'd brought them all the way from Nebraska and then took sick. He'd died a few days later on Mary's blue quilt, and they had buried him and sent the money for the calves to Jenkins's sister back in Lincoln, as he'd asked.

It had taken every cent they had, and Pedro, in his sly way, had pulled him aside and whispered, "*Capitán*, maybe you have no need to send the money. Maybe this old hombre's sister does not know exactly where he is traveling. She could not know he was crossing your land when he fell sick, could she? Maybe she does not even know he has these calves."

Teach vetoed that with a look. Pedro had shrugged, and he had never mentioned it again.

And now, four years later, Teach was heading home to a pregnant wife with his saddlebags full of money and his heart full of hope for a bright future.

He was a seasoned and careful traveler, and he and Salty, his good dapple-gray gelding, made it all the way up through Mexico to the border, and all the way to Tucson, where he bought Mary a new dress. It was to be a surprise, and he had to go to three stores to find just the right color. Robin's-egg blue, to match her eyes.

He'd never known another woman with eyes like his Mary's.

He left Tucson with Mary's dress in his saddlebags—along with a new plaited leather hatband for Rance and a supply of the best chewing tobacco for Pedro—and headed northwest, along the dry bed of the Santa Cruz River. He'd left Tucson far behind before he remembered that he'd bought nothing for himself. It didn't matter. He'd be home soon, and Mary was all he needed.

He moved northwest then, up through the Estrella Mountains, toward the Gila River. He was three miles from the river and ten miles from the ranch, only ten miles from Mary after two long weeks on the trail, when somebody shot him.

The bullet came out of nowhere, and he remembered suddenly tumbling from Salty's back, falling on sharp gravel and weeds just beginning to go brittle with the first real heat of summer, and discovering to his horror that he couldn't move. All this, before he heard the gun's report.

He lay there for what seemed forever, drifting in and out of consciousness, his body twisted and helpless and awash in pain, unable to make a sound or to force his watering eyes to blink. He couldn't even see the ridge from which he was certain the shot had come.

And he hurt, he hurt so bad! Pain was nothing new to

him. He'd nearly lost an arm in the Indian campaigns. He'd also been shot by a deserting coward at Fort Lowell, taken an Apache spear to the side at Granite Tanks, and broken both his legs when he fell from partway up Picacho Peak.

Of course, that Picacho Peak thing was stupid. He was just skylarking. But those injuries were nothing compared to this unending, pulsing agony in his spine.

He wondered if he'd ever see Mary again, if he'd die out here. He cursed the man who had shot him, for what reason he couldn't guess. Nobody up here could have known about the money he carried. He cursed the sniper for a coward, cursed him for not coming in to finish the job.

His eyes tearing from the sun and the pain, he watched Salty wander slowly from his range of vision. *Go home, Salty, go on home,* he thought. *Your oats are waiting.*

It wasn't more than ten miles. They'd send someone when Salty wandered in without him. Mary would cry and Pedro and Rance would backtrack the horse, and they'd find him. And then he wondered if they would realize he was still drawing breath, or if they'd bury him alive.

The sound of plodding hoofbeats came to him, rousing him from another near-swoon and up into bright pain.

Three men rode into view. They rode calmly, at a meandering walk, and stopped a few feet away. They had his horse. He could just see Salty's head at the edge of his frozen frame of vision.

They sat their horses silently, looking at him. And while they sat there, Sam Teach memorized their faces. He saw them as they were. He saw them cleaned up and filthy, shaved and bearded, dressed in Sunday suits and stripped to the skin. He made certain that he'd know them anywhere and in any condition, for what little good it would do him. The last face he'd see would likely be that of a hungry coyote. That, or a buzzard. They were already beginning to circle.

From atop his horse, the light-haired one of the bunch finally spoke. "He dead?" Stupidity dulled his eyes, and his voice broke with youth. Pimples spotted his forehead and cheeks, and under-rode the faint fuzz on his chin. He couldn't have been more than sixteen.

The older man mounted next to him—burly, flat-faced, his cheeks thick with dark stubble—leaned forward, bracing on his saddle horn. "Looks like," he announced through a mouthful of stained teeth, as distant from each other as pickets on a fence. He spat down into the low, sparse weeds less that a foot from Teach's face, then sat back with a creak of saddle leather. "Some piece'a shootin', Chambers."

Chambers, his brown, oily hair pulled back into a thick horsetail, said, "Nope, bad shot. I was aimin' for his horse. Don't see no blood."

The flat-faced man stepped off his mount.

"What you doin', Ike?" the boy asked.

He sounded just a hair nervous, and Teach thought, *I'll show you scared, you little sonofabitch,* before he belatedly realized that he wouldn't be showing anybody anything ever again.

"Gonna get his purse, you idiot," Ike replied, bending over him, blocking the sun. "Gonna get his gun, too. Too nice to leave."

Distantly, Teach felt the weight on his hip lessen as Ike slid the Colt from its holster, and then saw him again as he stood up and hefted it.

From his horse, the oily-haired Chambers called, "He double-rigged?"

"Don't think so," Ike replied, but he bent low again, grabbed Teach's shoulder, and rolled him all the way over on his back. The pain was immense, radiating outward in hard-edged waves. For a moment Teach felt his consciousness rolling away and the blessed blackness taking over, but it wasn't going to be that easy. His eyes watered a fresh gush of tears.

"Nope," said Ike, going through his pockets. "Just the one. And no goddamn money on him, either!" And then he peered into Teach's face. "Hey, Chambers?" he said, his sour breath wafting over Teach's face. "I don't believe you killed him all the way."

He put a hand on Teach's chest, and growled, "Shit! Still breathin'!" He stood up and leveled the Colt at Teach's chest. "Tommy Boy!" he barked. "Grab hold'a my horse."

The boy bent and snagged the reins.

"Wait."

It was Chambers. Teach didn't remember hearing him dismount, but suddenly he was standing overhead, too, his head haloed by the sun. He leaned down and prodded at Teach's body. New waves of pain emanated from his touch, and Teach wanted to cry out, *Kill me, you bastards, just kill me and get it over with!*

Chambers stuck the toe of his boot beneath Teach's shoulder and, with a little heave, rolled him halfway over again. "Thought so!" he heard Chambers crow. "Slug took him in the back. Likely got his spine. I'll be damned if he ain't still breathin'!"

"Told you," Ike growled, and leveled the Colt again.

Chambers slapped at his gun hand. "Put that damn thing away an' save the bullet. I already killed him. He's just gonna take a little longer to croak, that's all." And with that, he kicked Teach savagely in the back, at the site of the wound. The blow rolled Teach over twice and brought a fresh explosion of pain.

As he landed on his back, praying for death, a groan escaped him. It was a small groan, weak and feeble, but it was the first sound he'd been capable of making. His faltering lungs filled with air. He blinked his eyes once, then twice, and thanked God for the ability. And then he realized he could move his fingers. They felt full of tiny, biting things—half-numb at the same time—but he could wiggle them a little.

Chambers and Ike had joined Tommy on horseback again. They plodded past him, unaware that he could move his fingers, now his hands. And as they filed past him, his gray in the rear, he realized that there was a fifth horse tied to Salty's empty saddle, a horse he recognized as Pedro's old bald-faced Beau.

Beau's saddle wasn't empty.

Mary, dear God, it was Mary! Gagged, blindfolded, and tied into the saddle, her figure swayed limply from side to side, and her chin rested on her chest. Her dress was ripped and dirty. There was blood on her face.

Stricken with a horror so great that his own pain was momentarily forgotten, he moaned, "No!"

Frantically, he fought to make his legs move, fought to make his hands bear weight, to push himself up, to pull his Mary from that horse, to pull her to him and then kill every man of them for touching her, for hurting her. But his fingers only twitched uselessly against the pale ground.

And then he heard Ike say, "Aw, what the hell."

He looked just in time to see the smirk on Tommy Boy's face as Ike twisted in his saddle and yanked Teach's Colt from his belt.

He heard the report as Ike fired, and then the world went black.

2

King Garner was pretty much beat, but he was awfully glad to see the last curve in the trail to home come into sight. He'd been over to Gallup, selling some green-broke colts and fillies and a handful of yearlings, and he'd come out better than all right on the deal. A couple of hands from the ranch, Jim and Fred—actually, his only help, besides Hobie—had taken the string over to New Mexico along with him. They'd decided to make a stay-over in Zuni before they came out to the ranch, to home.

Frankly, he didn't much count on seeing them until to-morrow afternoon. The way Fred was making eyes at lit-tle Suzie Doorman, Mike Doorman's daughter from over at the town livery, maybe not until the day after.

It didn't much matter, Garner thought as he rode wearily yet happily through the towering pines, enjoying the cool mountain air on his face. He was fine, he had money in his saddlebags—enough to run the ranch for another year, and then some—and life was pretty damned good. He gave Faro, his big bay gelding, a pat on his glistening neck.

"Bet you'll be as glad to see your own stall as I'll be to see my rockin' chair," he muttered. "Least this was an easy trip. None of that running-your-legs-off crud."

The horse snorted and bobbed his head.

The last time he and Faro had ridden this way home, he'd had his arm in a sling, Hobie at his side, and they had just come from Prescott, where they'd dropped off a dead-for-three-days corpse at U.S. Marshal Holling Eberhart's office.

Of course, they'd been sporadically doing much the same things for three years now, ever since that deal with Belasco and Martindale. And ever since Holling Eberhart had ridden out, once it was done, and sworn him and Hobie in.

Garner grunted and shook his head. That damned Eberhart. Him and his shiny silver deputy U.S. marshal badges. It made sense that something like that would turn Hobie's head. He was just a kid, after all.

No, not just a kid, Garner corrected himself. Hobie had come an awful long way since that first trip. He'd got himself a bit of an edge, grown an inch and a half, and hardened up a bit. He was a pretty fair shot, good with horses, and he could damn near read Garner's mind. Garner would never admit it, but it halfway gave him the willies sometimes.

Hobie was good on the trail, too. Good? Hell, he was as good as Garner himself at tracking, although Hobie could see a lot better. No store-bought glasses for him, no, sir.

Damn the young, anyway.

Garner rode slowly around the last bend in the shady trail and came out on a large clearing—the stable yard. Hobie had been scything back the grass while he was away, because the place was neat as a pin. The big stable with its corrals was down to his left, the big paddock in between, and then the yearling barn up the hill a bit. It looked like old Hobie had given the paddock a fresh coat of whitewash, too.

The house was almost at the summit of the timbered hill, tucked into the edge of the surrounding pine forest. It was nothing fancy, just a simple house: a combined kitchen and dining room and parlor, and a couple of bedrooms. And the porch, of course. It was as wide as the house, deep-roofed, and his rocker and a table sat out on it, faced toward the big pasture down the hill and toward the setting sun.

Which it was just about getting time for.

Garner stopped at the barn and settled Faro in, and stopped to scratch Red, his stallion, on the nose. Red was officially retired from chasing bandits through the brush at high speed. He was too valuable as a stud. Why, just last year, Orin Swan, the biggest man in quarter-mile running horses, had made a special trip out from Texas to see him. And try to buy him, of course.

He'd offered Garner ten thousand dollars. Now, that was a bleeding fortune, and Hobie had just about passed out when Garner told Swan that there was no way he'd part with the stallion.

But after all, why should he? He had a ranch, he had enough money to get him by, and he had the best colts and fillies in the country coming up. That was worth more than all the cash money in the world to him.

He ran a hand down Red's neck, then slung his saddlebags over his shoulder and left the barn, heading up the hill toward the house.

"Where in the hell do you think you're going?" King Garner snapped. His saddlebags were still slung over his shoulder, his mouth was set for a lemonade, and he had expected that Hobie Hobson would not only greet him happily, but that the kid would pour him a tall glass and eagerly ask about the trip.

But no. There was Hobie, packing his bedroll and bags, and taking enough food to feed an army.

To make matters worse, when Hobie turned to answer him, Garner saw the glint of that damned deputy U.S. marshal badge on his chest.

"Holling Eberhart's been here, hasn't he?" Garner asked, and dropped his saddlebags on the table with a thud.

Hobie shrugged. "You just missed him," he allowed. "He said to tell you 'hey' if you wandered in before I left."

Garner tamped down his anger—or perhaps it was more like indignation that Hobie had been ordered out on a case and he hadn't—and pulled out a kitchen chair. He flipped it around and plopped down, his arms crossed over the back.

"What is it this time?" he asked, thumbing back his hat. He could be civil about this.

"U.S. Marshal Eberhart says there's been some trouble down south," Hobie said, pausing. He always said it that way. The "U.S. Marshal" part, that is. Hobie, all five-foot-seven of him, turned to face Garner. Hobie was still so blond that after the summer was done with him, a man would think at first glance that he was an albino, save for those piercing blue eyes of his. These last few years had filled out his wiry frame some, but he was still whip lean.

"Go on," Garner said.

"Don't need to growl at me," Hobie said, hoisting a pale brow.

"Wasn't," grumped Garner.

Hobie pressed his lips together for an instant, then said, "He just came for me, if that's what you were wonderin'. Already got a boss for this one, and he outranks you. Eberhart figures you don't like takin' orders."

Garner said, "He thinks right." Maybe Eberhart had some sense after all. "Who's running this thing?"

"U.S. Marshal Ned Smallie."

Garner stood up so fast that the chair beneath him toppled to the floor. *"Smallie?"* he bellowed, and Hobie was startled enough that he jumped backward, right into the kitchen counter.

"That jackass?" Garner added.

"Crimeny, Boss!" shouted Hobie, and looked down at the reddish mess slowly making its way down one leg of his britches as well as the curtained shelves under the counter. "You made me bust a jar of strawberry jam!"

But Garner wasn't paying much attention to broken jars. "What the hell was Eberhart thinking?" he shouted.

"I don't know!" Hobie shouted back. "I'm just followin' orders!"

A blob of strawberry jam slipped from the counter's edge and made a soft plop on the floor, punctuating the silence.

"Well, shit," Garner grumbled.

Hobie relaxed visibly, and began mopping up the mess with a rag.

"What's the case?" Garner asked, righting his chair.

"A lady got taken off," Hobie said. "A Mrs. Teach. Fellers stopped into her ranch—her man was away—and asked for water or somethin'. Ended up . . . takin' advantage of her. Before they took off with her, I mean. They killed both hands, too. Seems that Mr. Teach was on his way home, 'bout five or ten miles from the ranch, when somebody shot him. They figure it was the same ones who got his missus, on account of the tracks." He stopped to pick up a stray shard of glass, then swore and stuck his finger in his mouth.

"Rancher dead?" Garner asked. It sounded pretty hopeless to him. That rancher's wife was likely dead already somewhere out in the sand and brush. It was a sorry thing, but it was probably the truth.

"Nope," Hobie said, and pumped water over his hand and into the sink. He squinted at his finger, then gave a sniff. "Fella's in a coma, though, or so U.S. Marshal Eberhart tells me."

"And he didn't want me?" Garner asked.

"Heck, Boss, you never want to go anyhow! I figured you'd be plumb tickled to sit out on your porch and count your money." Hobie picked up a dish towel, then gave it a couple of turns around his finger. "How'd you do at the sale, anyway?"

Hobie hadn't exactly planned to leave that afternoon, but considering the way Garner was snapping at him and grumping around the house, he'd lit out early. A fellow couldn't get too far with only two hours of daylight to put under his horse's hooves, but Hobie figured to make it as far as Snyder's Pass.

Which he did, at just about sundown.

As he made camp and settled in Fly, his good buckskin gelding, Hobie thought over his meeting that afternoon with U.S. Marshal Holling Eberhart.

Holling had sat out on the porch, a glass of lemonade in one hand and his smoldering pipe in the other, and his head shaking in between. "Bad business, Hobie," he'd said. "Awful bad business."

And Hobie had asked if they shouldn't wait for Garner.

"Not with Ned Smallie around," Eberhart had said, just like Hobie should know what he was talking about. "Why, you and I both know that King Garner would have him dead in a ditch within five minutes of their meetin' up, and then I'd have to hang King. Sure hate to do a thing like that to a man like King."

And before Hobie could ask why there was such bad

blood between his boss and U.S. Marshal Ned Smallie, Eberhart added, "Wouldn't have sent Ned Smallie if I had my druthers, no, sir. That's why I'm sending you, Hobie. I want at least one good man down there, and since I can't send King, I'm sendin' you."

Hobie had lit up like Christmas. Now, he knew that Eberhart thought he did a good job. At least, he supposed Eberhart did, since a few years had gone by since Eberhart had pinned that deputy's badge to Hobie's shirt and it was still there. Hobie knew that he'd only been deputized in the first place so that Eberhart could get Garner's goat, and he still had a twinge of self-doubt now and then. But now Eberhart was sending him off by himself.

A good man, he'd said. *I need at least one good man down there.*

Hobie smiled.

He only wished that he hadn't been so swollen up with pride that he'd forgotten to ask about Ned Smallie. How had a man like Ned Smallie, who seemed to be universally reviled—at least by Eberhart and Garner, who were Hobie's universe, once you came right down to it—get to be in the position of U.S. marshal anyhow?

Well, Hobie supposed he'd find out soon enough. He could be down south of the Gila River in three days if he made slap time. And traveling on his own, he was bound to. Of course, Ned Smallie was already on the case, having lit out after those no-goods within two days, but Hobie figured that tracking Smallie, who was riding with a sizable posse, would be a piece of cake.

He just hoped that Smallie's boys wouldn't catch up with their quarry before he got there.

He had some sort of secret wish to be the one to save the day, although he probably never would have admitted that to anybody, least of all himself. But some part of him needed to prove himself, needed to do something grand and important without King Garner along.

When he'd first started riding with Garner, he'd done it because he wanted to see bold men doing brave things, great things. And he'd seen a heap of it, more than he'd counted on. He'd learned that bravery and true courage were most often a quiet kind of thing, and more often rose from being pressed between a rock and a hard place than from anything else.

The difference between a courageous man and a coward, he guessed, was that when things got truly desperate, the coward panicked. Brave men, like Garner, got real quiet inside and outside, too. Instead of breaking out in a cold sweat and getting crazy or scooting under the nearest rock, they figured that if they were going to die, they might as well do some good on the way out.

Hobie had a feeling that he was more like the latter example, and although on a few occasions he'd surely wished there was a potbellied stove to cower behind, he'd never showed cowardice.

He wanted to do it when somebody besides King was around, though. He didn't know how much of his bravado came from absolutely knowing that Garner wouldn't let him get killed.

He rummaged through his possibles bag and came up with fixings for supper: cold fried chicken, which he set aside; flour, baking soda, and so on for biscuits; a pot of blackberry preserves; and a pouch of Arbuckle's.

He measured out the Arbuckle's first, and set the coffee on his fire to brew while he mixed up the biscuits.

He imagined Ned Smallie lost out there, leading his posse around in circles. And then Hobie would ride up with the sun off his shoulder and glinting like fireworks off his holstered guns, all dramatic like in a play, and within five minutes he'd scout the area and hold up his hand. "Over here, Marshal Smallie," he'd call. "They went this way."

And off they'd ride.

Probably have the outlaws in hand that very night, and Mrs. Teach would be safe.

Hobie set the biscuits on to bake and shook his head. Poor lady.

3

Sam Teach woke in a dark place. He lay on a soft bed, and a worn quilt covered him. Without thinking, he ran a hand over the stitching and whispered, "Mary?"

And then the memory of it flooded back in on him, every detail, and he lurched up into a sit. Immediately, fire swept through him, its source in his back, in his chest.

He felt cool, dry hands cupping his shoulders, heard someone murmur, "No, you don't."

He passed out again.

When he opened his eyes once more, it was well into the day and he was alone. Lace curtains, drawn against a beating sun, filtered the harsh outside glare, and he could hear birds chirping outside. The room itself was soft yellow. A green-and-white bowl-and-pitcher set rode the washstand, and over the bureau hung a framed print of kittens, frozen in play with a ball of yarn. Beyond the door, he heard the unmistakable sound of bickering children.

He knew where he was. Somebody had brought him to Will and Bess Thurlow's place. He relaxed a little.

He pulled down the worn green-and-yellow quilt to take a look at his chest wound, but his torso was swathed in bandages. Fresh ones, too. Bess had been at him, and recently, by the looks of it. He was straining to sit up when the door opened.

"You're awake! You lie back down, Sam Teach," Bess scolded before she turned her head and called, "Jason, go fetch Papa. Tell him Captain Sam's awake."

"What time is it, Bess?" Teach asked. From the corner of his eye, he saw a shadow cross the curtains as Jason, the Thurlows' middle boy, scampered past the window toward the barn.

"Better you should ask what day it is," Bess said. She slid the tray she'd been carrying to the top of the bureau and came to him, pushing him back down with plump, gentle hands. Bess and Will were their closet neighbors, and blond, big-boned Bess was Mary's best friend. The two women always looked so odd when they were together: Mary so small and fine and appearing more delicate than she was, and Bess, her senior by ten years, so wide and comfortable and homey.

Bess's husband, Will, had been Teach's orderly. He'd mustered out two years before Teach, and had been the one who'd gotten him all stirred up about a future in ranching.

"All right, what day?" he repeated.

She held a hand to his forehead.

"Bess, let me up." He lurched up again, but his head commenced to pound and the room started swimming, and he fell back upon the pillows.

"Told you," she said, folding her arms over her broad bosom. "You're weak as a kitten. No fever, though, thank the Lord."

Angrily, he said, "You don't understand. They've got Mary!"

"Not for long, Captain," came Will Thurlow's voice. He stood in the doorway, casually blocking it with his sizable bulk. Like Bess, he was big and blond—although his hair was shot through with silver—and tall, well over six feet. His worn face was centered by an impressive handlebar mustache, and his thick neck drove down into shoulders as wide as a draft mare's backside.

Back when they were both in the cavalry, Will had topped out at 230 pounds. These days, years of Bess's good cooking had pooched his gut a few inches over a belt that looked as though it were ready to strangle him.

"U.S. Marshal Ned Smallie's on the case," Will added with a sizable degree of satisfaction.

"Smallie?" Teach said, and his heart sank. He'd met Ned Smallie once, the year after Will mustered out, when Smallie was a self-important little shit of a town sheriff. It sounded like Smallie had come up in the world, and fast. Probably still more interested in politicking and keeping his boots polished than in protecting the citizenry.

"He's from up Phoenix way," the big Swede said. He eased into the room and sat on the overstuffed chair beside the door.

"Don't you go putting all your weight on that chair, Will Thurlow," cautioned Bess, who was ferrying the tray from the bureau to Teach's bedside. "You know what happened last time."

"Hush, woman," Will said with a wave of his wide hands, but Teach noticed that he rocked part of his weight to his boots. "As I was saying, Ned Smallie, U.S. Marshal," he announced confidently. Obviously, he'd never heard of the man until a few days ago. "Course, we sent for Sheriff Becker and the doc right off when they brought you in, and—"

"Who found me?" Teach interrupted.

"Couple of Max Warner's boy, out after strays down south of the Gila. Getting about the time of year to move 'em up north. They found about a half dozen with your brand, if you're interested."

Bess wiggled a dribbly spoonful of broth in Teach's face, and he ate it just to make it go away.

"How'd Smallie get in on it? And what about Mary?" he asked with increasing urgency. "Did they get those vipers? Damn it, Sergeant, report!" He shouted the last bit, and immediately gripped at his chest. It felt like somebody was in there with a hot saber.

"You settle down, Sam, or I'll send Will from this room," Bess commanded. "You've been shot through the lung, as well as very near your spine. Doc Burton said it was a miracle you weren't paralyzed." She pointed the spoon at him like a gun. "How would that be, to just lie in a bed for the rest of your life, to have people come in to feed you and change your nappies? And roll you over, when they remembered it, so you wouldn't get bed-sores?"

His mouth set into a hard line and he didn't answer her. He'd already had a small taste of paralysis, and he hadn't cared for it one whit.

"This is the first time you've stirred since three nights ago, Sam Teach," she scolded. "I won't have you tearing out—"

"Three nights?" he asked weakly. That meant Mary had been in the hands of those animals for four days. His hands balled into fists around the quilt.

"Since you last woke up, Sam," she added softly. "You've been here nine days."

Dead. It had been too long, and Mary was dead. He squeezed his eyes shut against it, as if by blocking Bess and Will and this room from his vision, he could make it not be true. He would wake up any minute, and this would all be some terrible nightmare, some vast cosmic misunderstanding. Mary would be there, Mary with her soft brown hair and her robin's-egg eyes, and she would put his hand on her belly, and he would feel the baby move for the first time. He would feel life.

"Sam? You hurting?" Bess's voice intruded.

He kept his eyes closed. "Mary," he whispered.

He heard the clink of a spoon against glass.

"Doc left this for you, Sam," she murmured. "Come on, open your mouth."

With a cry of hopeless rage, he flung his arm to the side. He opened his eyes in time to see the spoon, spraying liquid, fly wildly across the room and bang off the wall.

Bess leapt back in a shock that immediately turned into a hopeless anger. "Don't you think I miss her, too?" she cried, her face twisting. "Don't you think I think about her all the time, about what she went through there at the ranch, about . . . about what those animals must have . . . how she must have . . ."

She broke into sobs, and Will went to her.

"Sorry," Teach whispered as Will led her from the room. "I'm sorry."

That evening, when Teach woke again, Will Thurlow was sitting beside his bed. Will marked his place in the book he'd been reading and set it aside. "Morning, Captain," he said in an attempt at cheeriness.

"It's not morning," Teach replied sullenly. Mary was dead. What did it matter? He rubbed at his face. "It's as dark as the inside of a black sow out there." He took a deep breath, inhaling the scent of Bess's rich beef soup, and winced when he took in too much air. "About Bess, Will. I'm sorry. I know she's hurting, too."

"She'll be all right. You ready for your report?"

Heat climbed up Teach's neck and settled into his

cheeks. "I apologize to you, too, Will. That was uncalled for."

Will shrugged, and his mouth crooked up into a half smile. "Old habits. I near about saluted. You reckon you're ready to hear it now?"

He nodded. He'd been ready this afternoon, too eager to hear a word, a hint, that she was still alive.

With a grunt, Will turned his chair toward the bed and began. "After they brung you here, I sent Jimmy for Doc White and Sheriff Becker, and I sent Clem out to your place to get Mary. Doc got here first. Captain, he said you likely wouldn't see the next day, but he did his best. Pulled a slug out of your lung. He dug and dug, but he finally left the one in your back. Said it was too dangerous. Said you'd need a specialist."

"Get to the part about Mary," Teach said softly. He didn't want to hear it, but he had to. He wanted Will to hammer home the point, make him believe she was gone. Because, for the life of him, even though he knew nine days was too long, even though he'd seen those pigs— and seen her, half-dead even then—he still couldn't make himself believe.

"I will," his old sergeant said. "You want a drink of water?"

Teach shook his head.

"Well, Clem came skidding his horse into the yard about then. I never seen him so shook up, Captain. After he got calmed down, he said he found Pedro shot dead up by your house and Rance barely alive down by the corral. He couldn't find Mary anywhere. Ol' Rance lived for a little bit, long enough to tell Clem what happened."

He paused and looked away, drawing those blunt fingers through his hair. "I'm not going to tell it easy, Captain. There's no way to."

"Say it out," Teach said thickly.

"They rode in about noon," Will said, and he was staring at his knees, not at Teach. "They asked for water and a meal, said they'd pay. They said they were going over to Yuma on business. Mary took 'em right in—you know how Mary is, Captain, she never met a stranger—and fed 'em good and said they had no need to show their money. And afterwards, after that blessed woman had cooked for 'em and poured their coffee and had Pedro grain their horses, they . . ."

Will's head dropped into his hands.

"Go on," Teach said. He had no need to steel himself, for he was already hardened to what he knew Will would tell him. He'd known ever since he'd seen her tied onto that horse half-senseless, with her clothing ripped and blood on her face. Sorrow pulled at his insides, but he shoved it away.

He reached over and rested his hand on Will's arm. "Go on, man," he said again, more softly.

"They did her bad, Captain," Will said quietly, his voice breaking. "They got Rance down by the barn, shot him in the gut, and they shot Pedro when he was running up to see what was wrong at the house. She was screaming, and . . ."

Will turned away for a moment, and all Teach could see was his Adam's apple bobbing over and over. Finally, he said hoarsely, "About an hour later, when they were done, they brought her out, trussed like a sack of feed and slung over the big one's shoulder."

Ike, Teach thought.

"They set out southeast, but before they did, Rance heard 'em talking. Arguing, more like. One of 'em wanted to just kill her and hightail it, but the other two said something about takin' her . . . taking her down to Galgo. They said, she's young and good-lookin', why kill her when she'd fetch 'em a pretty penny?"

Teach's belly lurched and his breath caught in his throat. Galgo. At last, he'd found a strand of hope. They were taking her to Galgo, to the rumored white slave auctions.

Will continued. "Sheriff Becker was here by then, and he heard the whole story, and what he said was, 'I've gotta catch Ned Smallie!' He jumped on his horse and galloped out of here before we knew what was what. Doc had to tell us that Marshal Smallie was passing through town, transporting prisoners to Yuma. The upshot was that Smallie left his prisoners in the care of Deputy Fletcher, and him and Sheriff Becker and a posse of ten men rode right out."

He turned toward Teach and leaned forward. "I wanted to go in the worst way, Captain. Would have, too, but Bess just wouldn't have it," he said with some embarrassment. "Said I had two spreads to take care of till you got on your feet, if you ever did again."

"It's all right," Teach said. If he'd been Will and Bess had told him no, he wouldn't have gone either. She was a formidable woman.

"Jake Boggs had to turn back on account of his mare pulled up lame, but he said they tracked 'em to where they'd shot you."

"Galgo," Teach muttered under his breath. "I just came from down around Galgo."

Will hadn't heard him. He said, "Deputy Fletcher heard the other day that two women had been taken from a ranch outside Silverbell. Three men killed, and a woman and her fourteen-year-old daughter gone missing. If those bastards are going to Galgo, that'd be pretty much on their way." He snorted. "Looks like they plan to turn it into a real moneymakin' trip. You know, right up until I heard that, I always thought those slave auctions were made up."

Teach tried to adjust his position, but the pain forced him down again. Grunting, he said, "You say the posse left nine days back? On the day I was shot?"

Will shook his head. "'Bout noon, the next day."

The door creaked open, and Bess stuck her head in. "Thought I heard voices. You up for some supper?"

"Thanks, Bess," Teach said. "Thanks for everything. And I'm sorry for—"

She waved a hand. "No need. I've got beef soup simmering. Sound good?"

He nodded and said, "I can smell it bubblin'."

"Just for you," she said, and closed the door behind her.

Will stood up. "Any day, now, they'll come riding in with Mary," he said, but the thread of sincerity in his voice was belied by his eyes. "You'll see, Captain. Smallie's a good man, from what I hear. Becker isn't much, but at least he's out there trying. And Bob Trevor's in the posse. He's as good in a fight as any two fellas."

Teach knew what Will wasn't saying. That if they were going to catch up with the trash that had taken Mary, they'd have done it by now. They'd have been back by now or sent word. Chambers and Ike and Tommy Boy were either hiding out, snaking through the desert, or else well past the Mexican border and traveling at their leisure.

Still, Teach said, "Thank you, Will."

Will sighed and shook his head. "Twenty years in the cavalry, Captain. Twenty years, and I've seen a lot of things that would turn any man's stomach. You seen 'em, too. But that was different, somehow. It was never anybody I . . ."

He broke off, but Teach knew what he meant. It had never been anybody Will had loved. Anyone who'd ever seen her, ever known her kind touch or heard her sweet voice, loved Mary. In the dead of winter or the blistering heat of summer, she brought the spring.

"I know," Teach said softly, and when Will didn't reply, he asked, "Doc say when I can get up?" It didn't matter. He knew he'd be up and out of here and on his way south the minute he could stand without fainting like a schoolgirl.

"Said another week or two, and then you gotta get straight up to Denver. Get that slug dug out of your back before it shifts. Doc's already written to the man who's gonna do the digging. Mary'll be back by then and she'll go up there with you. You'll see."

Teach looked directly at Will and held his gaze. "You think she's dead, don't you?"

Will paused a long time. Finally, he said, "I'm praying she's not." With that, Will left the room, and left Teach to his thoughts.

Teach didn't for one blessed minute envision that posse bringing Mary home, with or without U.S. Marshal Ned Smallie, no matter how much Will and Bess were hoping. Smallie had waited too long, had been gone too long. The Army had taught Teach that red tape and orders and the chain of command—especially when it was the command of some swollen-up shitheel of a U.S. marshal—had fouled up many a mission. He knew that Will Thurlow knew it, too.

Wishing wouldn't bring Mary back. Action just might.

He ate the supper Bess brought him and obediently opened his mouth for the medicine. He slept again, long and hard, and when he dreamt, his dreams were filled with hard revenge and cold anger.

But shining through it was the growing, glimmering hope that Mary could still be alive.

Hobie hunkered over his dinner plate, away from the others circling the campfire, and flicked at his beans with the tip of a bent fork. He could see why King Garner was reputed not to be on the best of terms with Ned Smallie.

For one thing, Smallie was an idiot.

Hobie had ridden down as double-time quick as he

could—that being four days—and once finding the posse's track, located the bunch of them in less than another day.

And for the past two days, he'd been doing nothing but ride in circles, following Ned Smallie's supercilious backside all over creation. At least, all the parts of it that they had no business going to.

Oh, Ned Smallie had listened to him for a bit. About as long as it took them to find the body of one of the rapists, a boy Smallie had called Tom Something-or-other. The kid's body was there with them now, wrapped up in blankets at the site of their camp. He was already stinking and maggot-ridden when they found him, and another day on the trail hadn't helped rectify the situation.

After that Smallie ignored Hobie's at first quiet—and then more pointed—suggestions as to which way, exactly, they should go.

In fact, Smallie had sent them off in the exact opposite direction from where the tracks led.

Sheriff Becker, who was the local law down around where Mrs. Teach had been kidnapped, said nothing. Hobie couldn't figure out if he was just too dumb to see those tracks, or whether he was just too dazzled by that U.S. marshal's badge on Smallie's chest.

Hobie had been at first, but he sure wasn't anymore. Dazzled, that is.

In fact, he was just about ready to ride off into the night, go back to the last town he'd seen, and send off wires to both U.S. Marshal Holling Eberhart and King Garner. He'd tell Eberhart what he was doing and why, and he'd beg Garner to get off his backside and come down here. He could use a hand, all right.

Why, if he'd had Garner along, they'd have had those boys in custody already, and those ladies—it was *ladies* now, not lady, he thought ruefully—would be back at home, where they belonged.

But his duty tugged at him painfully. This was the first time he'd ever been sent out alone—the first time he'd ever served without Garner along, that is. And he, Deputy U.S. Marshal Hobie Hobson, was going to call it quits? Something in his gut told him to tough it out, that Smallie knew what he was doing.

But the wiser part of him said, *Leave and leave now, Hobie, time is of the essence.*

And anyhow, Smallie was just a tin-hat lawman who made the late Marcus Trevor—another U.S. deputy who had turned out to be the biggest publicity-seeking horse's backside Hobie had ever met—look like Allan Pinkerton.

Hobie stood up, leaving his tin plate of beans on the ground. That was another thing. These boys were the worst kind of cooks, and on top of that, they wouldn't let Hobie near the campfire.

Well, he wouldn't go near it, anyway. Too close to that rotting body.

He wondered for a minute if maybe he shouldn't tell Smallie where he was off to. But then he stood there, watching Smallie at the campfire, showing off with those stories again, and decided against it. Smallie would probably call him a deserter, but too bad.

Hobie scooped up his bedroll, hefted his saddle, and set off toward Fly and the picket line, out there somewhere in the darkness.

And when he rode out, unnoticed, he didn't even bother to tip his hat in Smallie's direction.

4

Word got around that Sam Teach was conscious, and the people started coming. The McCallister brothers, who worked for Max Warner at the Rocking W, and who had found him while gathering strays, were among the first. They came while Doc White was there, and Teach thanked them for saving his life.

"You couldn't'a been lyin' there too awful long," Roy McCallister said quite seriously. He turned his hat between thick fingers and added, "The buzzards wasn't lit yet."

Shyly, his little brother, Rich, offered, "They was circling in thick, though."

"It's a miracle you idiots didn't do him in yourselves," Doc said angrily. "Tossing a man in his condition over a horse! Jesus Christ Almighty!" He dipped his gray head, put his ear to Teach's chest, and said, "Breathe as deep as you can, son."

"Well, you didn't kill me," Teach said quickly, for the McCallisters both looked stricken, "and that's a fact."

Then he sucked in a deep breath for Doc, and was immediately sorry. It felt like something had ripped inside, but Doc nodded and said, "Good."

"No, sir, Sam," Roy said quite seriously, "I guess we didn't."

"Again," said Doc.

"You're the one who's trying to kill me," Teach hissed through clenched teeth. "Evil bastard."

"Shut up and breathe," said Doc. "And you McCallisters wait outside. Scat!"

Doc White checked the wound in Teach's back with approving grunts and hums, had Teach wiggle his fingers and toes, and made him follow his moving finger. At last he sat back and said, "You usin' the chamber pot on your own yet?"

Teach nodded. He'd been as embarrassed as hell at the alternative.

"Well, don't go any farther than that for a few days," Doc White said, "even if you feel like it. That slug in your back is as close a call as I've ever seen. Miracle you didn't go numb and stay that way from your chest down."

"Oh, I felt it good enough," Teach said, frowning. "Couldn't move a muscle—hell, I couldn't even blink!— till one of those cowards booted me in the back. But I felt it the whole time."

Doc raised a craggy brow. "You felt it?"

"Like sin. Doc, I never had such pain in all my life."

Doc shook his head. "One for the record books, Sam." He snapped his bag shut and got to his feet. "Next week, we'll get you up to Denver and Dr. Jarvis. He's a good man. The best there is for this sort of thing. And Sam?"

Teach waited. He knew what was coming by the look on Doc's worn face.

Doc said, "I sure was sorry to hear about Mary and the . . ." He looked away, cleared his throat, and added, "It's a hard thing, Sam. If it's any comfort, I know what you're going through. I lost my Sarah over thirty years ago. It was during the War. Lawrence, Kansas. She was staying with her sister when those low-life cowards, Quantrill and Bloody Bill, rode in and took the town."

Doc's voice had grown thick. He stopped, and Teach was thinking that it never stopped hurting. Some wounds defied healing.

Softly, Teach said, "That's a tough thing, Doc. I'm sorry."

Doc lifted a hand and said gruffly, "No gallivanting, young man." And then he was gone.

Doc White had given up on Mary, had given her up for dead. Even Will had skirted the mention of her name since their talk that first night. They had all written her off—sadly, of course—but written her off just the same. She had gone to Galgo, over the border, gone deep down into Mexico. And as far as any of them were concerned—even Will, even Bess—that was the same as dead.

Not Sam Teach, though.

Sam had become increasingly certain that she was alive. He had to believe. He couldn't do otherwise. He'd almost given her up at the beginning, but that wasn't a mistake he'd make again.

And he'd lied to Doc. He wasn't just shuffling the three feet to the chamber pot.

Each night he'd walked around his room, stood in the by-God middle of it, and raised his arms over his head, done deep knee bends, and even a few faltering touch-your-toes. The first time he'd tried that, the pain had been so intense that he'd passed out.

Luckily, he'd fallen sideways, onto the bed, so there wasn't much clatter. At least, it hadn't awakened Will and Bess. And when he'd come to, he'd started all over again.

He could almost pick up the bedside table—and everything on it—without screaming.

He gave himself two more days.

Two days until he'd be able to hoist that table—about the same weight as a saddle, he reckoned.

Two days before he could leave to fetch Mary home.

The afternoon before Teach's planned exodus, a tired and ragged posse rode into the Thurlow ranch. Two men, Rosie Tate and Phil Cooper, put Teach in a wooden chair and carried it out into the yard, and Bess shooed the kids inside the house.

"Heard you're an ex-military man," said U.S. Marshal Ned Smallie. It was obvious he didn't remember Teach, but Teach remembered him. Smallie was short and thick—a good bit thicker than the last time Teach had run into him—but despite the dust and grime of his journey, he was still so full of himself that Teach wanted to take a swing at him.

Smallie puffed out his chest, looked down his nose, and added, "I reckon you can take this, then." He signaled to one of the men, who led up a horse, its saddle bearing a burden covered by a tarp.

The unmistakable stench of death preceded it by a good ten feet, and the boys who'd carried Teach from the house held their noses and backed off. Flies swarmed thick around the horse's sagging load.

"The bastard's pretty ripe," Smallie said with too much humor for the situation. "I was going to take him straight to town, but I thought you might like to see him 'fore we plant him or he falls to pieces. Whichever comes first."

With that, Smallie flung back the edge of the tarp.

"Holy cow!" came a young voice from house.

And behind him, Teach heard Bess shout, "Jason! Jimmy and Joseph! You pull your heads back inside and say the Lord's Prayer this instant!"

A window slammed. Teach didn't look around, though. He was staring at the body.

The man had been dead a long time, and when Smallie grabbed him by the hair to pull his face up and show it to Teach, part of the scalp came away in his hand. Fat maggots roiled in the blackish ooze beneath. They fell to the ground in twos and threes to wriggle in the dust.

Muttering, "Jesus H!" Smallie flung the bit of scalp away, then repeatedly wiped his fingers on his trousers.

Teach, however, was unmoved. The air about him was a pool of stink, but still he sat there, expressionless, staring at the corpse and listening to the angry buzz of flies, and beneath it, the muted sound of three distant and childish voices reciting, "And lead us not into temptation, but deliver us from evil . . ."

"Tommy Boy," Teach said at last.

Smallie, still staring at his hand, said, "Somebody cover him up an' lead him outta here 'fore he gets the whole place to reekin'."

Belatedly, Sheriff Becker swung a leg down off his horse. "How you doing, Sam?" he asked with genuine concern.

Teach didn't answer. He was watching Walt Soderfeld tether the horse down by the barn.

"Jumped the border, by God," announced Smallie, "but we got one of 'em."

"You mean *they* did," said Becker in disgust. "Must'a had themselves a scrap, Sam. We found him where they'd camped one night. Stabbed in the back. Boy'd been dead a while."

Teach didn't much care. "And Mary?"

Becker crouched down to Teach's eye level. "Sam, hard as it is for me to say, forget about her. You gotta just get up and go on with your—"

"Will!" Teach roared, so hard that his wounded lung felt like it had burst, and so loud that Becker lost his balance and stumbled backward. And when Will appeared directly, he wheezed, "Take me inside."

• • •

Later, when the posse had left, Will knocked at his door.

"Filter it out for me," Teach said.

Will leaned against frame. "You sure?"

Teach nodded tersely. "The pertinent details."

"Feel like I should be wearing my blues," Will muttered before he began. "It goes like this. There were three men, like you said. Tommy Fogel's the one that got himself dead. The other two are Milt Chambers and Ike Smeed."

Tersely, Teach nodded. He already knew their names.

"Chambers used to be a scalp hunter," Will went on, "but lately he's mostly taken to robbing pilgrims up and down the Colorado. There's a couple of murder charges waiting for him in Yuma, and another up in Wyoming, someplace. He's got a reputation as a real sharpshooter, too."

Will scowled. "Now, Ike Smeed's a horse of a different color. Not much on him, except that he knifed a man over to Tubac last fall, and there was some bad business about a girl down in Buckworth a couple years ago. Becker thinks he's been operating mostly in Mexico."

"And the Mexican authorities?"

Will snorted. "Which ones? Hell, Becker said Smallie didn't even bother to check. Or try to. Not that it matters. You never can get much that makes sense out of those fellas. But I guess I was wrong about Ned Smallie being such a good man. Even Becker was just plain disgusted with him, and if *Becker's* disgusted with somebody, you just know they've gotta be lower than a snake's belly."

"Doesn't matter," said Teach. Smallie was out of it now. "What else?"

"They only crossed the border three days back," Will said. "I guess they led that posse a merry chase, circling all around in the desert. And besides those two women they picked up in Silverbell, they've got another one. Saloon gal. Grabbed her right from under Smallie's nose outside Bisbee. You ask me, I think they did it just to piss him off."

Only three days ago. They'd head straight for Galgo, but now that the posse wasn't pressing them, they'd likely slow down, take their time.

"And Mary?"

"She's still with 'em, Captain. At least, they're leading four horses."

Then Will looked at him, really looked. He let out a sigh, and slowly shook his massive head. "All right. When do we leave?"

"Not we. Me."

"Now, Captain . . ." Will began.

"No," Teach said, cutting him off. "Bess and the kids need you. Besides," he added, smiling just a little, "who else is going to take care of my ol' Turnip bull while I'm gone?"

Will stared at the floor for a moment before he met Teach's eyes again. "When you leaving?"

"In the morning," he said, and when Will opened his mouth, he added quickly, "I'm fitter than I look."

"Yeah, I know," said Will. "Didn't figure you were payin' somebody to come in and move your furniture at night."

In spite of himself, Teach felt heat seeping into his cheeks.

If Will noticed, he didn't comment. He stood erect. "Take my Shorty. He's a good horse, and he'll get you there. I'll have a pack ready and your clothes laid out for you in the morning, Captain. Wouldn't do to tell Bess. And Captain?"

"What, Will?"

"A couple more things. That posse had a man riding with them for a few days. Becker said he was a deputy U.S. marshal from up north somewhere. Said it was on his account that they found the body in the first place, but that he hightailed it a couple nights later. Smallie's gonna report him for deserting, but Becker figures that he'd just had enough of Smallie, because he didn't take off up north. Said his tracks were heading straight back to Bisbee."

Teach just stared at him.

Will sighed. "Well, I just figured maybe he was gonna wire for help, or go after those boys on his own, that's all. Becker said he was a trackin' fool."

"You said two things," Teach said, his expression unchanged. Some fool of a deputy, U.S. or no, was neither here nor there.

Will said, "All right. The posse found your old Salty horse stone dead no more than half a day's ride from where those polecats left you. Looked like he'd stepped in a hole and busted his leg. I'm right sorry."

Teach rose at a quarter to four the next morning. Will, ever the efficient orderly, had put out clean clothes for him, and left a bedroll and plumply packed saddlebags. He'd also laid out Teach's gunbelt. Will's worn Peacemaker, the spare he kept up over the mantel, was in the holster.

Teach shrugged into his clothes, hissing only once when he moved the wrong way and his back gave him a sharp twinge. He gobbled the thick roast beef sandwich that Will had left for him, gulped down the buttermilk, gathered his bedroll and saddlebags, and then quietly crept through the house.

Once outside, he moved quickly for a man in his condition. Shifting the saddlebags to the side that hurt a little less, he walked to the corral and eyed its drowsing horses, but Shorty wasn't among them. The barn, perhaps. He slid open the door to find a lantern lit and Will waiting with his arm crooked over a stall rail.

"Mornin'," he said with a grin. "Thought you'd lie in bed forever, you lazy bastard."

Two horses—Will's dark bay, Shorty, and his tall cremello, Butter Pie—, were saddled and waiting, and Teach shook his head. "You're not going."

"Yes, I am," Will said stubbornly. "I should'a gone with the posse. Maybe that good-for-nothing U.S. marshal would have caught up with 'em if I'd been there to push him."

Teach slung his saddlebags up on Shorty. "No."

"You can't tell me 'no,' Captain," Will insisted. He could be a bullheaded sonofabitch sometimes, and he was surely showing his horns now.

"I'm going, all right," he went on mulishly. "I'll dog your trail if I have to. What if your back goes bad all of a damn sudden? Doc said it could happen any time. What if you fall off ol' Shorty here and can't move, and there's nobody there to pull your fat outta the fire?"

Teach snugged the saddle strings around his bedroll. Will had already tied a bloated water bag to the horn, as well as two canteens.

Teach put a foot in the stirrup. "You try to follow me, Sergeant Thurlow, and I'll shoot you in the foot."

"Oh, no, you won't, Sam Teach." They both turned toward the open barn door to see Bess, her hair in a long, thick, blond braid that snaked over the shoulder of her blue tartan robe. "He's going."

"Honey?" said Will meekly.

"Honestly!" she said, scowling. "You men. Do you think you could both go tiptoeing out and I wouldn't hear you? Me, who's heard the sneaks and rustles of three children doing mischief?"

"Now, Bess, honey . . ." Will began, but she cut him off.

"My Will is going with you, Sam. No ifs, ands, or buts. I'm only sorry I didn't let him ride with the posse."

Her mouth tightened into a line. "Enough said about that. I'll send Jimmy to turn out your livestock and bring Turnip back here, and Clem can go water your truck patch every other day. And you, Sergeant Wilfred Thurlow?"

She walked up to him, and Will—who in his career had fought Indians and whites and red tape and the occasional deserter, who had been wounded countless times, and who was among the bravest men that Sam had ever known—cowered just a little.

But Bess threw her strong arms around him and kissed him hard on the mouth, and Teach heard her whisper, "Come back to me, Willie Boy. Come back, or I'll have your guts for garters."

5

By the time Will Thurlow and Sam Teach set off to find Sam's wife, Garner was already almost halfway to Bisbee.

Hobie's telegram had come, all at once so strident and disjointed that it didn't sound like Hobie at all. If nothing else, Garner planned to get down to Bisbee and rattle some sense into that boy's head.

He was just south of Phoenix at the moment, heading down toward Tucson. It was barely dawn, but he'd been in the saddle for over an hour and it was about time for him to take a little saddle break and switch horses.

He'd brought two, taking it easy on them, switching off every hour or so. Right now he was riding Faro, the good copper-bay gelding that had seen him through more than one scrape, and leading Pepper, a tall but pretty blue roan mare that he'd bought the spring before to breed to Red, his prized stallion. Except that the mare had come up barren.

It was a damn shame about that. She was a good horse, nearly as surefooted as Faro, and quicker on the rein if that were possible. Well, he had let Red cover her again this spring. Too soon to tell if she was in foal, but Garner figured that this early on, it wouldn't hurt her any, either way, to put some miles under those hooves.

He reined in Faro and dismounted, then watered both horses. "Yeah, I know it's hot," he muttered to Faro as the gelding lipped water. "Blame it on Hobie." Pepper nudged him from the side. "Hang on, gal," he added with a smile. "Your turn's coming right up."

He was more worried about Hobie than he let on, even to himself. It was the kid's first time out on his own, after all. Garner was so worried, in fact, that when he'd got the telegram, he'd scribbled a quick reply that said, COMING STOP GARNER, and had thrown a saddle over Faro before the messenger from town had left the yard.

He suspected that he got halfway down to Horse Thief Basin before that damned telegraph boy got back to town.

Of course, it didn't hurt that things were a little slow around the ranch. It was just the excuse he needed for a little dustup.

And he'd been thinking about that lady, too. Wondering if she was mercifully dead. He'd known a lieutenant named Teach once, a long time ago. Maybe it was some kin of his. Garner didn't really think so. This shavetail had been fresh from back East somewhere. A West Pointer, or some such. He'd probably served out his commission and gone on home. Most men did—at least, those that survived—when they were sent to serve in Arizona during the Apache Wars.

It was more than likely just a coincidence. The Apache Wars were long over, Geronimo had been packed off to Florida, and Lieutenant Teach and scores of his brothers had probably gone back home.

He finished watering Pepper. She must have been named for her looks, not her temperament, for she was as sweet as rock candy. He patted her on the neck, checked her girth, then mounted up.

He sat there for a moment, taking in the colors in the early morning sky. Purples, reds, pinks, oranges, and coppery russets all vied for a place in the sky, and for just a second he wished he was a painter, if only so that he could give those colors their right names. Calling that orange color *orange*, for instance, was an insult to it. The Good Lord must have some kind of palette, all right.

And then he caught himself at it again, thinking old men's thoughts about things like colors, and snorted under his breath.

Leading Faro behind him, he set off for the south at a ground-covering jog.

Mary Teach's hands were bound, and she was tired, so tired.

Still, she managed to loop her arms about Becky Lowell's shoulders and pull her close. The girl was scared senseless, and she'd been that way for the past week. They all were scared, but this child was only fourteen.

The child's mother, Agatha Lowell, had neither spoken a word nor raised a hand since the night these men had ridden into their ranch. They had murdered her brother, her husband, and a ranch hand, then raped Agatha over and over while Mary cowered in her bonds and tried not to hear her pleas and screams, and those of Becky.

Agatha had fought like a madwoman at first, trying to shield her daughter, but a mouse had more chance against a trio of hungry barn cats than Agatha had against these fiends. It had been useless. She now bore two black eyes and a broken nose for her trouble. Her dress had been literally shredded to the waist, and hung down in strings.

Right away, Mary had laboriously torn a good-sized piece of cloth from her own soiled petticoats, thinking that Agatha could wrap herself in it. But the poor woman was past the point of caring. She'd lost the cloth within two minutes, letting it flutter away on the breeze, and had possessed nothing but her thin, bound arms to cover herself for days. Bruises, scrapes, and scabbed bite marks covered the fair skin of her torso, which was by now badly sunburnt and peeling. She sat across from Mary and Becky, hunched into a ball. Her broken nose was swollen closed, and she breathed loudly through her mouth, staring into space, a comfort to no one, not even herself.

It was dawn, and Mary thought they were somewhere in Mexico. Their captors had hardly confided in them, but they'd slowed their pace considerably in the past few days, which meant they were no longer being chased.

"It's all right, Becky," Mary whispered into the yellow tangle of the girl's hair. She was blond and blue-eyed and pretty, like her mother. Like her mother had been, before Ike Smeed used his cruel fists on her face.

Mary soothed the girl's temple. "It'll be all right," she repeated.

Faintly, Becky whispered, "I want to die, Mary."

Nellie Sykes, a girl of perhaps twenty-two or twenty-three years, sat beside them on the hard ground. Her hands were tied like Mary's, and her spine was pressed resolutely against a rock. A petite brunette with hair as black as a raven's wing and large, expressive, coffee-brown eyes, Nellie had been the last woman the men had kidnapped, while she smoked a cigarette in an alley behind a Bisbee whorehouse. Mary had never imagined she'd be able to find the least thing to admire in a soiled dove, but Nellie had changed her mind.

In her tough but fluty voice, Nellie whispered, "No, you don't, kid. You don't want to die. You want to live to see these sonsabitches hang. You want to live to spit on their goddamn graves."

Becky began to cry. Again.

While Mary rocked her, Nellie hissed, "Stop it! I don't know how you lasted so long with these shitheels, cryin' all the time!"

"Shh," Mary breathed, as much to Nellie as to the weeping Becky. "Hush. You'll wake them up."

Agatha continued to stare.

Shrugging, Nellie held her tongue, and Becky snuffled quietly into Mary's shoulder. No one wanted the two men to wake any sooner than necessary.

It had been a week and a half since that awful day they'd come to Mary and Sam's ranch near the Gila. In that short span of time, Mary had gone from resignation to anger to horror and revulsion—and back again—a thousand times over. She had learned not to fight them when they took her. She had learned that the rape was as inevitable as it was terrifying and degrading. But it wasn't the worst thing.

The worst thing would be losing her baby.

And so she had stopped struggling, because when she struggled, they beat her mercilessly. She already knew that she had broken ribs. She felt them each time she took a breath. She just closed her eyes and lay still and prayed the Lord to keep her unborn child safe.

She was only about two months along. Not far enough to show, not yet. Not far enough along that anybody but her Sam would have noticed. She had kept her mouth closed on the subject, even to the other women.

Sometimes she wondered if these men would have taken her if her pregnancy had been more advanced, if she'd been ungainly and waddling. Would they have eaten their meal and gone on? Or would they have raped, then killed her?

It was a moot point. She was with them now, and she

was bound for the auctions at Galgo. They all were. She'd heard them talking.

Each day, while they were looping and twisting all over the Arizona desert to evade the posse, she had kept an eye to the horizon. Sam would come, she told herself. Sam, her own personal pirate.

She'd always teased him that he must be descended from that scourge of the seas, the great Blackbeard himself, old Edward Teach. Sam had the last name and the coal-black hair to prove it, didn't he? But he always just clucked his tongue at her and, winking, said, "Fetch me another tankard of ale, wench!" or some silly thing.

Sam would come. She'd known in her heart that any moment he'd be riding down to get her. Maybe he'd bring the cavalry. He hadn't been mustered out that long. They'd remember him. They'd have to remember the former West Pointer who had served with such valor during the Apache Wars!

Or perhaps he'd come with a posse from town, maybe that posse these filthy swine had been evading, although the men in the posse had been so stupid and ill-fitted for the job—even these illiterate fools had run rings around them!—that she soon decided that Sam couldn't be among them.

But he'd come even if he had to come alone, and he'd come soon.

Except that he hadn't. And now she feared that something horrible must have happened to him, because something horrible was the only thing that could keep Sam from charging after her.

Near the fire, Milt Chambers, his oily horsetail swinging, stood up and stretched against a dawn sky of pink and orange and deep purple. Such a beautiful sky to have such an ugly man standing before it.

"Shit," whispered Nellie. "He's awake. I'd give anything for that pig-sticker of Ike's."

So would Mary. But while she was fairly certain that Nellie's first thought would have been to use the knife on their captors—in various gruesome ways, which Nellie had detailed to pass the time—Mary would have cut her bonds and ridden away from Milt Chambers and Ike Smeed just as fast and hard as she could.

She hugged Becky tighter.

As usual, Milt Chambers made water beside the fire. He didn't even possess the manners to turn his back. His urine hit the ground in a hard stream, splattering the boots of his sleeping partner.

They had killed their third member, the one they called Tommy Boy, five nights ago, just one night before they'd kidnapped Nellie. It had been a fight over poor little Becky Lowell, and Ike Smeed had knifed Tommy Boy twice in the stomach and again in the chest, and then slit his throat, just to make sure.

Mary had felt no sorrow at his death, no sorrow at the gruesome manner in which it had come. She had felt nothing at all, except relief that now there were only two men to torment them instead of three.

Milt Chambers didn't bother to button his trousers. He merely walked over, stared at them for a moment, then pointed to Becky.

"You," he said. "Blondie. Get up here."

Becky tucked her head into Mary's shoulder and began to wail. It was a high, keening sound, nearly animal in quality except for the mantra-like "No no no no no . . ." that only Mary could make out. Mary held her poor, insulted body closer and glared up at Chambers.

Chambers swore and bent to grab the girl, but then Nellie's bound hands shot out to grip his forearm. "What's the matter, cowboy?" she asked, her conversational tone belying the fear and hatred that Mary knew was in her heart, in all their hearts. "Can't you handle a real woman so early in the mornin'?"

Chambers took hold of Nellie instead, and hauled her to her feet. "Sure," he said, and yanked Nellie's torn dress aside to plant a rough hand over her breast. "You want it, don't you, whore?" He stuck out his wide tongue and licked her bruised face from jawline to temple in one broad sweep.

Nellie shuddered visibly, but through clenched teeth, she said, "That's right, baby, that's right."

He smiled. "I wanted me somethin' with a little more gumption to it," he whispered, before roughly, he pushed her back to the ground. He reached down, shoved Mary's protecting arms away, and hauled a hysterical Becky to her feet.

"Please!" she screamed as he began to drag her toward the fire. "Please don't! Mama!"

"Drop her, Chambers," came Smeed's voice. He was on his feet. "If I don't get to, you don't either. Didn't you tell me as what she'd bring more if she wasn't touched?"

Chambers paused, then pushed poor Becky to the ground. "You gotta remember everything, don't you?" he asked in a surly voice. He pointed to Nellie. "All right. Come on, whore."

Later, when Chambers was finished with Nellie, and after Ike Smeed was finished with her, too, Mary fixed their breakfast. It was the only time they removed her ropes. Since Agatha was frightened past the point of knowing where—or who—she was, and since Nellie didn't cook and Becky could do little more than cry, the meal preparation had fallen to Mary.

She did it quietly, as always—her head down, her movements slow—calling as little attention to herself as possible. It was the same every morning. Pancakes made with powdered milk and powdered eggs and mealy flour, served with sugar syrup from a can. There was bacon, too, rancid bacon that she and the other women didn't eat, but which the men packed away. It only underscored her opinion of these animals. Like hungry wolves, they could and would eat just about anything.

She poured the batter into the pan, which was sizzling with lard. It helped to mask the sound of Becky's sniffling, but not enough, it seemed, to please Chambers.

"Shut the hell up back there!" he yelled. He was slouched on the other side of the fire from Mary, his head propped on one hand, his filthy horsetail dragging in the dust. "Shut your damn mouth or I'll really give you somethin' to wail about!"

Beside him, Ike Smeed sat against a rock, toying with his boot knife, the one Nellie called a pig-sticker. "Thought you said as how we wasn't supposed to hit 'em no more, Chambers. Bruises'll bring the price down in Galgo."

Chamber slid Smeed a look, but then closed his eyes against the morning sun and sighed. "Reckon it will. 'Sides, you been bangin' them around more than me. But damn, that yeller-headed little bitch just won't shut up! I'm sick an' tired of hearin' her whine."

Ike chuckled. "Well, I reckon she'd cut it out fast enough if you was to stop pokin' her mama every five minutes and start pokin' her instead. You're such a handsome fella, too, what with that hangy-down horsetail'a yours."

Chambers grunted. "Them flapjacks ready yet?"

"Almost," said Mary. She tried to make herself invisible. She tried not to think about the small burden, weighing heavy in her pocket.

"Well, hell. Why don't you go ahead and switch on over to the little gal?" Ike went on. "Yeller hair, 'bout the same build. Course she's a kid, but I don't see as how it makes much difference. I mean, you al'ays take 'em from the back anyhow."

Chambers stiffened. "And what's that supposed to mean?"

Ike stabbed his blade into the ground between his knees, then raised his deeply tanned hands and held them wide. "Nothin', nothin' at all," he said coolly. "I was just sayin'. Just didn't seem to me you'd know the difference once you got goin', that's all."

"Screw you," growled Chambers.

Mary lifted the first two pancakes from the skillet and slid them onto a plate, then poured more batter into the pan. She kept her movements slow and small. Her ribs hurt too much to breathe otherwise.

"Mine," Ike said and grabbed it, as well as the tin of syrup. He was in such a rush he nearly knocked over the coffeepot.

"Jesus, Ike," said Chambers, who put a hand out to save the coffee. "Tapeworm actin' up again? How many days, you reckon?"

"Till Galgo?" Ike said around a mouthful of flapjacks.

"No, till Christmas, stupid."

Smeed frowned. "You're the one what's been there before."

"Hell, Ike," Chambers said, "you got us so damned turned around I don't know where I am anymore."

Glaring, Ike said, "Four, maybe. I know exactly where we are. And I ain't got no tapeworm, and I also ain't stupid. You'd best watch your mouth." He shoveled another huge bite of flapjacks between those stained, picket-fence teeth.

Mary shuddered despite herself. *Oh, Sam, Sam! If you're coming, you'd better come quick!*

"Where's my goddamn flapjacks!" Chambers demanded.

Quietly, Mary said, "I'm cooking as fast as I can." Little bubbles were thick on the surfaces of both pancakes, and she flipped them over. She reached for the other skillet and said, "Bacon's ready."

She forked half the pan onto Chamber's plate, then half onto Ike's outstretched tinware. Four slices each of the smelly stuff. She hoped they'd get food poisoning and die, or at least get good and sick.

"Well, why don't you switch over to little Mary, here?" Ike said, and Mary's breath caught in her throat. "She's right pretty, and she don't fight none. Why come you don't fight no more, Mary?"

She kept her eyes down. Pancakes to the plate, more batter to the pan. *Don't think about the knife in your pocket.* "What's the point?" she whispered. Batter went into the pan with bacon grease, too. The more rancid food they ate, the better.

"See there, Chambers?" Ike crowed. "Got her trained! Well, we should keep that Becky gal pure-like for the auctions."

Chambers swallowed and washed it down with a long swig of coffee. "I like it when they fight."

Mary busied herself with cooking. Now the men received only the pancakes cooked in rancid bacon grease. The others, she set aside for the women. In days past, she'd dropped the men's food in the dirt when they weren't looking. She'd spat in the pancake and biscuit batter, and she would have peed in the coffee if she'd had a chance. And a week ago, she had tried to sneak a larger knife into her skirt pocket.

That time, it hadn't worked. Ike had caught her less than fifteen seconds later, and slapped her so hard that her teeth rattled. And then he had raped her yet again to underscore his point.

Mary shuddered. This time, she would be more successful. She had been so far, anyway. She'd had the knife for nearly ten minutes, and no one was the wiser. But if Ike caught her this time, he would surely kill her.

She didn't look at her pocket, even though she desperately needed to reassure herself that the little blade was still there, the blade she'd used to cut up the morning's bacon, then pretended to drop back in the pack. Ike had been watching, but she'd palmed it.

The only thing Mary had to be grateful for, other than the fact that she was still breathing—if painfully—and that her baby was all right, other than the fact that they hadn't yet discovered the theft of the knife, was that for Milt Chambers and Ike Smeed, the newness of their captives seemed to be wearing off.

Even the sickest man grew weary of beating a dog, didn't he?

From the beginning, when they had stopped their horses and pulled her, screaming and pleading, from the saddle seven or eight times between every sunrise and sunset, the rapes had presently dwindled down to three a day, sometimes two. Nellie was taking the worst of it, now that the new had worn off Mary and they'd bludgeoned Agatha into a comatose state. Not that they cared.

And despite what Ike had inferred, no one had touched Agatha since the day after they'd kidnapped her, although Chambers still liked to ride next to her during the day and pinch her nipples or slap at her sunburnt, peeling breasts. Agatha didn't care. She didn't even know he was there.

Perhaps she was the lucky one.

"Hurry up!" barked Ike.

Quickly, Mary picked up the spatula, lifted the last two pancakes from the pan, and put them on the stack. She picked up the plate and, still staring at the ground, said, "May I?"

Ike said, "Do it fast, then get your ass back here and clean up."

She rose, grabbed the coffeepot and the one cup they would share, and moved toward the waiting women.

Kneeling, she handed the plate to Nellie, then quickly transferred the little knife from her pocket to Nellie's.

"Atta girl," whispered Nellie as Mary poured the coffee. "It won't be long now."

6

Will rode a little behind the Captain, watching him closely. The Captain wobbled in the saddle every once in a while, something he'd never do if he were fit, but other than that he appeared perfectly normal. He still bore watching, though, and watching close. A man as stove-up as Captain Teach had no business in the saddle, let alone riding all the way down into Mexico.

"What are you doing back there?" the Captain barked.

Will moved Butter Pie up next to Shorty and fell into step with him. "Nothing," he said.

"Stop checking on me," Captain Teach said testily. "I'm not some baby, damn it. I'll tell you if my back gives out." And then his face softened a little and he shook his head. "Didn't mean to snap at you. Besides," he added, rubbing his chest, "it's hell on my lung."

Will thought it best to change the subject. "How's Shorty workin' out for you?"

"I'd know better if you'd let me move faster than a snail," the Captain replied.

Will rolled his eyes. "If you don't stop grumpin' at me

every two minutes, I'm goin' home. And I'm telling Bess what a sonofabitch you are."

Suddenly, the Captain's mouth quirked up into a smile. "Anything but that, Will."

They rode on, keeping their pace to a fast walk. Will insisted. It was easier on the horses, easier on him, and more importantly, easier on the Captain.

But so far, Teach hadn't evinced any sign of pain, other than the whiteness that had come over his face. That worried Will. He said, "'Bout time for another slug of laudanum, Captain?"

Unlike previous occasions, he didn't hear any back talk from Captain Teach. The Captain just grunted, then pulled the bottle from his pocket and uncorked the top. Will watched while he took a long pull on it and tucked it away with a grimace.

"Nasty stuff," said the Captain.

"So they tell me," said Will.

It was past noon. They'd crossed the Gila much earlier in the day, and were following the dry bed of the Santa Cruz, headed generally south. Despite the fact that they were holding their pace to a brisk walk, they had already covered a pretty fair distance.

Shorty, unlike his name, was a big, long-legged gelding, and Butter Pie, the cremello Will was riding, was perhaps half a hand the taller of the two. Will's horses had to be big. He was a big man, and Bess always teased him about having a corral filled with giraffes.

He smiled. That Bess was a doozy, kissing him like that, right in front of the Captain, and then slipping him a paper package with two big slices of her good dried-apple pie. He and the Captain had eaten it with their lunch, scraping the last sweet, gooey filling from the brown paper with their fingers.

He made a mental note to stock up on sweets in Tucson—what Bess didn't know couldn't hurt her—and also on laudanum. The Captain didn't have much left, and it sure looked like he was going to be needing it for some time to come. Poor bastard. If those peckerwoods had come through Will's place instead, if they'd taken his Bess . . .

Will couldn't think about it without his eyes burning and his throat getting thick.

If he'd been thinking straight, back there at the very first, he would have ridden to Tucson, to the cavalry. Surely they would have sent out a few men! He didn't think too highly of the Army, not anymore, but it would have been worth trying. Except he hadn't been thinking very clearly right then, what with his best friend and the finest man he knew lying senseless in his spare room, and U.S. Marshal Ned Smallie talking big.

He should have known better. That posse had been nothing but show from beginning to end. He should have known right off that Smallie was full to the eyes with horse dung.

But he hadn't, had he? Now it was up to him and Captain Teach, and they were a week and a half late in getting started. Plus which, if you asked him—and Bess and Doc and everybody else—the Captain should still be flat on his back.

Will hated like hell to make the admission, even to himself, but he knew they were never going to find Mary. If she wasn't already dead, she was surely well on her way to Galgo. They'd never catch up in time, not even if they rode down there at a dead gallop.

And the men who bought women at Galgo weren't looking for cooks or housemaids or seamstresses.

He loved Mary Teach like a little sister, but God forgive him, he hoped she was dead.

He felt a touch of heat pushing at the back of his eyes, and straightened in the saddle. Right now, he had to ride the Captain down into Mexico, and make certain he didn't kill himself getting there. Will knew in his heart that Captain Teach wouldn't be satisfied, wouldn't believe, until God just smacked him in the face with the truth of it.

Of course, God had already banged him up pretty good, in the form of those stinking kidnappers. That wasn't enough to take the heart out of the Captain, though.

Will believed in God. God was good sometimes, very good. But God did some downright terrible things, or at least, He let them happen.

Will had seen more evil in his time than any man should. He was an Old Testament man down to his bones, and firmly believed that the Almighty was a real blood-and-thunder deity, full of vengeance that He could hand down unto the seventh generation and beyond. Man was born, he suffered, he did the best he could, and he died. If he had some good times in between, it just meant God was busy thumping some other poor bastard for the sins of his great-great-great-granddaddy.

But the Captain? He and Will had never exactly talked things over, but he'd always had the feeling that the Captain saw things differently. Captain Teach held things to a higher moral level than most men, and back when they were in the Army, he had commanded by example. His hand had been quick, but always kind, and some of the men had called him weak. Until they saw him in battle, that is.

In Will's eyes, there had never been a braver man. He'd served with the Captain first at Fort Bowie, back when Teach was a lieutenant fresh out of the Point. At Fort Bowie, they'd protected pilgrims and supply trains wishing to traverse the treacherous Apache Pass—they'd seen some times there, hadn't they?—and they'd been transferred to Fort Lowell, where they'd chased Geronimo all over hell and gone under General Crook and, later, General Miles.

He'd seen the Captain put his own life in peril countless times to haul a wounded trooper back to the safe shelter of a rock or a wagon. He'd seen him fight hand to hand with the great Cuchillo Hierro himself, and sink his blade into the Apache's murdering heart. And he'd seen him stand up to that blustering, self-important idiot General Miles.

Still, there was no eye for an eye or tooth for a tooth for Captain Teach. Although on occasion, Will had known him to come pretty damned close.

But he had a feeling that should they ever catch up with Ike Smeed and Milt Chambers, Captain Samuel Teach was going to come through with some serious Old Testament retribution.

He honestly didn't know whether he wanted to see that or not.

Down in Bisbee, Hobie was having a rough time of waiting. When he'd received Garner's wire, he'd been so happy—not to mention relieved and edgy and excited—that he could barely stand it. In fact, he went straight from the telegrapher's office to the Needy Bird Café and had himself a steak dinner and a beer to celebrate Garner's impending arrival. He even stopped worrying that the U.S. Marshal's Service might hang him, or worse, for deserting back there.

But by the next morning, the beer and the steak had worn off, and all those fried onions he'd had with them had near-about taken over. At least, that's what he thought it was. But as the day wore on and his bowels had done their worst, he stopped being distracted by emergency trips to the outhouse and got down to some serious worrying that Garner still wouldn't get there in time.

Two times, he'd walked clear down to the livery, intent on saddling up old Fly and taking off after those bastards alone.

And both times, all he'd done was to give Fly a good brushing, talking to himself the whole time, and maybe brush Fly a little more firmly than he needed to.

Waiting was sure a tough thing to do. He was more used to just saddling the horse and getting the job done. Except this wasn't a one-man job, was it? Ruefully, he admitted to himself that it just might be, if that one man happened to be King Garner. But he wasn't Garner. He might have his own U.S. deputy's badge, but when you got right down to it, he was just a hired hand, just Garner's sidekick.

And he figured he'd rather be a live sidekick than a dead fool. So much for pulling something off all by his lonesome.

He waited.

Around five, his stomach got to rumbling—although in a good way, not like when he'd been sick from the onions—and he took himself back up to the Needy Bird. He plopped into a chair at a table in the corner and had a look at the blackboard menu.

The waitress recognized him. "Same as last night, mister?" she drawled.

"Yeah," he said. "But no onions. Them things gave me the trots somethin' horrible. Spuds instead."

She nodded. "Must'a been bad," she said as she walked away. "Half the town's been down with the epizootics."

Will and Teach camped that night on the eastern slope of the Estrellas, near the waterless bed of the Santa Cruz, and Sam Teach was thinking that rivers were funny things. The Santa Cruz, for instance, ran underground most of the year.

Teach had been told by old-timers down in Tucson that

long ago it had surfaced there—as well as several other places—year-round. There'd been swamps down in Tucson with game aplenty and good fishing, they'd said, and if you didn't let the whine of mosquitos drive you mad, or if you didn't come down with malaria or fall to the Indians, it was a pretty fair place to live.

But now? Too many men, too much livestock, and rampant irrigation had taken their toll. Now there was nothing. Dry as a bone.

It struck him that he had a lot in common with that river.

Or maybe it was just the laudanum doing his thinking. He'd taken a long swallow—well, two—not that long ago, and it had kicked in with a vengeance.

He was more exhausted than he'd ever admit to Will. Thanks to the laudanum, the fire had once again receded from his chest and back. But he still had a real hell-bitch of a headache, despite the medicine. Maybe because of it.

He'd thought about just tossing the laudanum away, getting rid of the damned brain-numbing stuff, but that idea didn't last long. Without it, the pain simply overtook him. He knew that with no laudanum, it would only be a matter of hours before he'd be curled up in a ball on the desert floor calling for his ma.

He heard a sound behind him, boot steps crunching gravel and low brush.

"Hungry?" Will asked, and handed down a tin plate swimming with beans.

He took it. "Bess should have come along," he said more thickly than he expected. He eyed the beans, and what he thought were supposed to be biscuits. He prodded one with a numb finger.

Will chuckled and eased his bulk down beside Teach on the riverbank, then picked up a stone in his wide fingers and tossed it down upon the rocks. It clattered loudly, momentarily filling the night air with sound.

"Some river, huh?" Will said. He tossed another stone. "I remember when this stretch used to carry water pretty near all year-round. The Pimas and the Maricopas used to farm around here." He pointed out into the night. "You look close, you can still see some'a their irrigation ditches."

Teach squinted, but couldn't see anything. It was too dark and he was too full of dope.

"Course," Will added, with a grin, "that was way back, when I first come out here. Reckon you were in grade school about then."

Teach didn't say anything. His tongue was as thick as his brain. He managed to locate his lips, and forked some beans between them. His mouth was numb, and the beans were tasteless.

"Captain? Can I see your medicine?"

He groped for his pocket, and finally found it. He thumbed out the bottle and handed it to Will.

Will held it up to the moon's light, and Teach heard him mutter, "Damn!" before he pocketed it. Will said, "I think from now on I'd better hang onto this, Captain. Damned if you don't push yourself till you're ready to drop, and then you take too much." He paused for a moment. "You're getting beans all over yourself, there."

Teach nodded. He tried to eat some more, but he had no appetite. Why had that pie at noon tasted so good when he couldn't taste this at all?

Will said, "It ever bother you, me callin' you Captain all the time?"

Teach shook his head. His shirt was now peppered with beans that had fallen from his fork, and he brushed at them ineffectively with his free hand.

"Reckon by rights I should be callin' you Major." Will went on. "But you didn't get that promotion till after I was mustered out. Couldn't call you Sam, not after so long. And Major just felt kinda funny in my mouth, you know?"

"S'all right," Teach said thickly. He knew that Will was just talking to fill the air.

The two men sat in silence then, Teach trying to eat what for all the world tasted, to his numb senses, like warm wallpaper paste. At last he gave up. His shirt was full, anyway. Half asleep, the plate in his lap and slowly spilling soupy beans onto the ground, he spoke at last, and with great difficulty.

"We're going to find her."

It took all the strength he had to say it. It was all he wanted to say, as much to Will as to himself.

"Sure, Captain," Will said. Mercifully, he didn't look over at the miserable wreck Teach knew he was. Instead, Will's gaze rested dully on the dry riverbed. "Sure we will," he repeated.

7

Will and Teach reached Tucson in the forenoon, and after Will stocked up on laudanum and foodstuffs, he and Teach boarded the train. Will hadn't been to Tucson in a couple of years, but what little he saw of the town as he scurried through his errands gave him hope.

Not that it was clean—which it wasn't, not with all those dead animals lying in the streets, flies abuzz—and not that it was much more civilized than the last time he'd seen it. But it appeared to be getting bigger all the time. It seemed to him there were more womenfolk around, too. White ones, and not just whores. They looked to him like wifely types. As his Bess always said, you've got to have plenty of white women to get a place civilized, and it looked like Tucson was getting in its fair share.

A few more, and they'd likely have the streets half clean.

At the depot, he left the Captain on the platform, then saw to Shorty and Butter Pie and got them settled in a boxcar. He then made his way up the train to third class,

located the Captain, and slumped into the seat next to
him. Just in time, too. He'd no more than gotten comfortable—well, as comfortable as a big man could get in
those skinny-ass seats—than the steam started jetting
and the conductor started shouting, "All aboard! All
aboard!"

The Captain seemed oblivious to it all. He was awfully
pale, and he sat, not looking out the window, his chin
practically on his chest, staring straight ahead at the
empty seat across from him.

Will knew it wasn't the laudanum, this time, that had
knocked his friend so low. Will was riding shotgun over
that stuff for the time being. He guessed that he'd be in
an almighty daze, too, if he'd been shot up and had his
wife raped and kidnapped and his hired hands murdered.
And he guessed that if Teach wasn't sozzled on the opi-
ate, then he was lost in the physical pain that never went
away. Not to mention the everlasting sorrow of it.

He suspected that the last part was the worst.

With all his might, Will wished that there was something more he could do to ease the Captain's agony. But
there wasn't. Not now. All he could do was what he was
doing. Just go along, just be there.

He was all but convinced that they were going to find
sweet little blue-eyed Mary dead, even if it was the last
thing he'd admit to the Captain.

Teach seemed to perk up a bit, or at least enough to
ask, "Horses all right?"

"Yeah," replied Will with an enthusiastic nod. "Got
lucky, Captain. They've got a boxcar all to themselves.
Straw was already down on the floor, and I gave 'em each
a flake of hay and a half measure of oats."

Teach nodded exactly twice. "Good," he said, and then
went blank again, went off to wherever his mind had been
before. Likely a good bit further south, where he imagined Mary to be.

They had left Tucson behind by this time, and were chugging south through the desert, past distant low mountains. Not a human person in sight, Will thought. He was glad to be out of the Army, glad to have a good, solid home with Bess and the kids. Will had more than once said that if he ever got the urge to wander off into the desert looking for Indians again, that Bess could just shoot him.

Well, this wasn't Indians, was it?

He sighed. No, the way he saw it was that he was just going to search for a body. It was a pitiful errand, and one he would not have done for any living person, save the Captain.

Well, and Bess.

With a thick finger, he pointed out the window, past Captain Teach and toward a curious sight: a rider, making a good pace on an easy-loping copper-bay and leading a second horse. The blue roan was a spare, if Will was any judge. It was saddled, anyway, and didn't look to be burdened down by excess supplies.

"Look there," he said, and waited until Teach's nose followed his finger.

By that time, the train had nearly caught up with the rider, who was about thirty feet off to the side. He rode loose and easy, not like a trooper, but like a cowhand. The Captain had always said that the Army trained men to sit a horse like they had steel rods up their asses, and Will was inclined to agree. "Sits a horse like a cavalry man," he added, hoping to get some argument out of Teach.

But if Teach had any response to this, he kept it to himself. Instead, he squinted and leaned forward a little, staring out at the man's face.

"Couldn't be," Teach said as they passed the rider. He shook his head and sat back—very slowly and very carefully, Will noticed.

His brow furrowed with worry, Will dug into his pocket for the laudanum, uncorked it, and passed the vial to the Captain. "Time for a sip?" he asked.

Teach didn't reply. He just took the bottle.

By the time they got down to Tombstone that evening, Teach was feeling better. It had helped that Will had loosed his grip somewhat on the laudanum, but the time spent on the train, despite its rattles and bangs, had helped ease his back. There was something to be said for resting in bed, after all, or at least something close to it. Right now, Teach was wishing there was a straw mattress he could sling over Shorty.

But still, he felt quite a bit better, not only in body, but in heart. He was closer to Mary now, closer to finding her. Closer to extracting his revenge on those animals.

He and Will had debated the Bisbee issue at great length that afternoon. Will was all for taking the train south, and Teach supposed this was to keep them both off the horses a little longer. But in the end, Teach won out. They were headed south, all right, but not so far south as Bisbee, and certainly farther west. In the long run, they'd get to their destination faster if they simply rode for it.

Of course, old Will hadn't counted on continuing on tonight.

"What?" Will said as he ripped the gingham napkin from his collar. "Have you gone daft?"

They were the lone patrons at a café at the edge of town. Tombstone had shrunk quite a bit since the mines flooded a few years back, and the place was a lot calmer, too. Actually, it was nearly a ghost town, compared to the way it had been in its heyday. Oh, there was still a girl or two up at the Birdcage, and the Presbyterian church seemed to be doing adequate business. At least, there had been a sign posted on it that they were holding a baked-goods sale next Saturday, but that the baseball game had been canceled.

The place was a shadow of its former self, though.

Will was glaring at Teach, his napkin wadded up in his fist.

"You heard me," Teach said. "I'm rested, you're rested, and the horses are rested," he calmly insisted, even though his back was paining him, and he knew it would be hurting a lot worse after a few hours in the saddle. "There's plenty of moon. And we both know this neck of the woods like the backs of our hands. We lounged around too long on that train," he added.

Will didn't say anything for a long time. He just sat there, working his broad fingers on that napkin, practically rubbing the red checkered pattern right off it, and then he suddenly threw it down to the table.

"If Bess were here, Captain," he said, "she'd take you to the woodshed, officer or not."

Teach managed a smile. "She's not here, though, is she?"

Milt Chambers and Ike Smeed were camped not far from the coastal town of Galgo. They had been fighting all day, arguing and occasionally taking a poke at one another. Mary had fervently hoped that one of them would become so enraged that he'd kill his partner—after all, it had happened before, with Tommy Boy—but so far, her prayers had not been answered.

They had killed Nellie Sykes yesterday morning.

Ike had found her with the little knife Mary had stolen, found her just slithering out of her bonds.

Stupid of Nellie to try right then, Mary thought. Stupid of her not to wait until night, until they were asleep. But Nellie was set on it, and after all, Chambers was busy with the horses and Ike was busy eating breakfast. Nellie had said she'd waited too long already, and it had taken her the whole night to saw her way through her ropes.

Ike had slit her throat, of course. He'd shown no more emotion than a man at a hog-butchering, even though Nellie had put up a good fight.

But what chance had she had?

What chance did any of them have, really?

And Mary was so numb from everything, from the constant fear for her own life as well as those of her sister captives and the trepidation of what was to come, that when Ike killed poor Nellie, Mary hadn't made a sound except for a low, half moaned "No" that no one heard.

Little Becky Lowell had screamed, though. Screamed as though she'd never stop. That is, until Ike slapped her to the ground.

The death of Nellie was what Chambers and Smeed had been bickering about all day. Chambers chastising Smeed, Smeed telling him to shut up. Chambers taking umbrage at that, then Smeed threatening him.

And vice versa.

"Look what we got left!" Chambers had shouted, then pointed toward Agatha, a bottle of whiskey hanging from his hand. "A walkin' ghost, and the blue-eyed gal's bruised up like a street brawlin' field hand." Then he'd pointed to Becky. "And one prime, 'cept she's bruised up one side and down the other, too!"

"You bruised 'em just the same as me," Ike Smeed had slurred right back. "And you fuddled the old one's head same as me, too. I ain't taking no blame for nothin'!"

"Least I didn't kill none of 'em," Chambers had growled. "You goddamn, hot-tempered sonofabitch. I ought'a slit *your* damn throat!"

They had scuffled, but it was nothing serious. Unfortunately. They had too much hootch in them by that time.

The men had finally stopped arguing and fighting and had mercifully fallen into a drunken sleep, leaving their captives uncomfortably trussed like three piglets on their way to market. Along with Becky and the vacant Agatha, Mary slouched in the moonlight, trying to find a comfortable position, trying to convince herself that her Sam was still coming, still looking for her.

It was getting harder and harder.

At least there had been no rapes since before breakfast. Ike Smeed was so mad about Nellie—and Milt Chambers was so furious with Ike for having done them out of the money she would bring—that they had done little more all day than snipe at each other, and hadn't even bothered to question where Nellie had gotten the knife. Their bickering was what had saved the women from further insult.

Mary hoped they'd continue to fight all day tomorrow.

Beside her, Becky Lowell, who now knew more of the ways of evil men than any girl of fourteen should know, whispered, "Tomorrow, they said. Mary, what's to become of us?"

"I honestly don't know, honey," Mary soothed. She had some idea, having overheard Ike and Chambers discussing their fate. At least a few sentences worth, until Ike caught her at it and backhanded her. But she wasn't about to share her fears and suspicions with Becky. They were far too horrible.

"Do you think we're in Mexico?" Becky asked softly, as a coyote gave voice in the distance.

Mary shivered at the sound. "I suppose," she replied. "We've been going south an awfully long time." Over two weeks, she thought. She'd been gone over two weeks, and still no Sam.

"Your husband," Becky said after a pause, as if she were reading Mary's thoughts. "Your husband isn't going to come for us, is he." Her voice didn't break. She sounded matter-of-fact, but tired, so tired.

Mary broke a little inside, though. Her voice thick, she

said, "He's coming, Becky. He'd just had a little trouble, that's all. I don't know what. But he's coming for me. For us."

She heard Becky sigh, long and hard, then mutter, "He'd best hurry, then."

8

By ten the next morning, Garner had broken camp and ridden a good twenty-five miles before his mare picked up a stone.

Cursing, he slowed himself down from an easy but brisk lope, which had been his favored gait for this trip where the terrain allowed, and set into a walk, riding Faro and leading the roan mare.

He was just coming up over a shallow rise when he heard it. And smiled.

He clucked to Faro and apologized to the mare, sped up into a jog, and breasted the top of the rise.

Yes, there it was. He hadn't imagined it. There was a train, just pulling up to a water stop in the stark, hard middle of nowhere. And it was headed the right way, too.

As he rode down toward it, the train, with a great sound of complaint and iron on iron, pulled to a halt. Three men scrambled out, and one was halfway up on top of the car and the second halfway up the water tower ladder before they sighted Garner riding down.

Garner lifted an arm and waved. These boys tended to

be on the nervous side, and he wanted them to know he wasn't out to rob them.

Still, the ones up top of the train and tower froze, and the one on the ground, just a young fellow, swung his rifle's nose out toward Garner.

Garner rode on up, though, and touched the brim of his hat when he came to a halt. He introduced himself, then showed them his badge. This wasn't exactly official business, but the badge did come in handy for something.

"Roan pulled up lame," he said, indicating the mare. "Be obliged if you could find me some room in a stock car. You're going south to Bisbee, aren't you?"

All three men visibly relaxed, and while the first and second pulled the big spout over from the water tower and lowered it into place, the third waved him down the train, toward a series of three boxcars. A moment later, he trotted after Garner, opened a car door, and pulled out a wide ramp.

"She's empty, sir," he said eagerly, as Garner led the horses up into the shade of the boxcar. "All yours. You wanna ride up front? Got a passel of seats left in first class."

But Garner shook his head. "I believe I'll take a nap instead, son," he said, pulling the saddle from Faro's back. There was no reason the horses shouldn't relax, too. "There's not much in the way of lyin'-down places in the passenger cars till night."

"Yessir, Deputy," said the boy with a grin, and slid the ramp up. "I'll come get you when we make Bisbee."

Once the train had jerked into motion once more, Garner finished pulling the tack off his horses, and then checked Pepper's hoof again in the stripes of dusty light that pushed between the rattling boards of the walls. She was all right. She just needed some time to rest up without anybody on her back.

While both horses fixed their attention on the narrow

hay-filled manger, Garner stretched out on the car's floor and pulled down the brim of his hat to shade his eyes.

He couldn't sleep, though, despite all his intentions to the contrary. Of course, the constant noise and rattle didn't help, but that telegram from Hobie was the worst. It kept on bumping at his thoughts like a pissed-off bull at a corral gate. He just couldn't help feeling that he was in for a whole lot more than picking up an addled hand.

Well, he figured the mystery would be solved in two, maybe two and a half hours. That was how long he figured the train would take to get to Bisbee.

He tried to concentrate on nothing more than the black on the inside of his eyelids.

"Goddamn it, Captain, just let me help you up!" Will thundered.

Sam Teach let himself sag against the saddle. His back had been bothering him more than usual, and now he found that he couldn't even mount his horse without help.

They'd ridden most of the night, camped for a few hours, and had then been moving again by dawn. Even Teach had to admit it was probably too much for him.

But then, whatever Mary was going through had to be so much worse.

"Give me some more of that poppy juice, Will," he said, his face leaning against the saddle leathers. He found he didn't even have the strength to turn around. Struggling to get his foot up was what had taken it out of him, he supposed. He'd been all right when they were eating lunch. Or maybe he turned wrong when he retightened the girth.

It didn't matter. It was sure as certain hurting now.

The bottle—along with Will's meaty hand—appeared before his face, and he accepted it and took a slug.

"Go easy, Captain," Will said gruffly. "That's your second dose in as many hours." Will had been harping at him for about five minutes to let him help mount up, but even Teach admitted—if only to himself—that he was stubborn. He was by God going to get on that horse and go. Except that he hadn't.

Teach swallowed the bitter liquid and handed the bottle back. "Just give me a couple of minutes," he said. His forehead was still against the saddle, against a crudely made steer's head tooled into the leather. Funny he hadn't noticed that before. Of course, he'd been sitting on it, he thought with a half-snort. He wondered if one of Will and Bess's rambunctious boys had put it there.

"Take all the time you want, Captain," Will said obligingly. Teach heard him walk back to his horse, heard the rustle of his saddlebags as he replaced the bottle.

Teach wondered just how much of that joy juice Will had bought in Tucson. At this rate, he'd use up a gallon before they got to Galgo.

Gradually, he straightened and rubbed at his forehead. He had a feeling there was a child's idea of a steer pressed into it.

"Let me give you a hand, Sam," Will said from behind him.

"I'll let you give me a boost, Will," Teach grumbled. "You don't have to go calling me Sam." He raised his leg and felt Will lock his hands under his knee.

"Just wantin' to keep on your good side, Cap," Will said with a chuckle in his voice. "One, two, three!"

Teach found himself suddenly in the saddle, looking down at Will. "Thanks," he said.

"You're welcome. You're white as paper, you know. Why don't we—"

Teach shook his head. "No. We can't waste any time."

For just a moment, Will looked as if he was going to speak, then seemed to think better of it. He walked over to the far side of his mount and swung his bulk into the saddle. "Whatever you say," he said. "You're the boss."

• • •

Garner found Hobie in Room 4 at the Alpine Hotel, which had been named, it seemed, by somebody who thought he was funny.

"Boss!" Hobie exclaimed after he answered Garner's knock. In fact, the boy was so jubilant that for an instant Garner was afraid that the kid was going to throw caution to the wind and hug him.

Wisely, he didn't.

However, he hurriedly stuffed his things into his saddlebags, snatched up his bedroll, and said, "Let's get goin'!" before Garner had a chance to step into the room, let alone sit down.

Hobie pushed past him into the hall, but Garner grabbed his shoulder and spun him around.

"Whoa up there, boy!" he said as Hobie's boots slipped out from under him and he started a quick slide down toward the floor.

Garner held him up by his shirt, though, at least until Hobie got his feet under himself again. Then Garner let go and said, "You want to let me sit down for five minutes first?"

Grudgingly, Hobie picked up his saddlebags up from the floor and reluctantly followed Garner back into the room. It wasn't much, Garner noted, even by Bisbee standards. One small bed with a ratty bedspread, one straight-backed chair, one badly silvered mirror, and one beat-up dresser. This last item was missing a leg, propped up by a stack of seed catalogues, and topped by a cracked washbowl and chipped pitcher.

Garner had seen plenty of rooms just like this over the years, and he was no fonder of them now than he ever had been.

"This the best place you could find?" he asked as he swung the chair around and sat down, his arms folded over the backrest.

"Huh?" said Hobie.

He just stood there, shifting his weight from foot to foot, and finally Garner growled, "Sit down, will you? You're making me nervous."

Hobie slouched down on the bed.

"And let go of those damned saddlebags," Garner added. "I don't plan on getting up for a spell. This is the first time I've sat on something that wasn't moving in a few days, and I kinda like it."

Hobie gave a small sigh of complaint, but he put his bedroll and saddlebags on the mattress beside him and crossed his arms.

"Better," said Garner. "Now, what's the big toot?"

Hobie rolled his eyes. "Boss, I told you! We got to get after those fellers! Heck, they're probably down into Mexico by now!"

Garner dug into his pocket and produced a folded piece of paper, which he held out at arm's length. He squinted for a second, then said "Shit" and reached into another pocket for his glasses.

With them perched uncomfortably on his nose, he read. "COME NOW STOP POSSE CRAZY STOP WOMEN ALIVE STOP HURRY NEED HELP STOP H HOBSON." He refolded the paper and removed his glasses, saying, "Now, what kind of a lunatic telegram is that to be sending me? You gone clear daft, boy? Hell, I half expected to find you strapped to a cot in the loony bin."

Hobie had the good sense to look a tad embarrassed. "Well, I was all het up," he said apologetically. "But that doesn't mean that I . . . Aw, heck. She's out there, Boss, and she's in trouble, and you should have seen that lunatic posse I was ridin' with! That Smallie ain't worth a bacon breakfast to a steer, and those boys he had ridin' with him were kowtowing and scrapin' and . . . Aw, cripes."

Garner could imagine what riding with Smallie's posse had been like. If there ever was a glory-seeking idiot, Smallie was it. Of course, Marcus Trevor had been a real showman, too, but at least he'd been brave when push came to shove. Not so Ned Smallie. Hobie must have been frustrated as all get-out.

But so much time had gone by! If the kidnappers hadn't killed her by now, they'd likely have beaten and abused her to the point that she didn't know her own name anymore.

Almost kindly, he asked, "You still want to go out after her, Hobie? It's been a spell. Maybe she doesn't want anybody to come after her."

The look on Hobie's face told Garner volumes and also made him a little ashamed, but Hobie added to it, saying, "Boss, those fellers what took her, this Smeed and Chambers, they're animals. There was three of 'em at first, them two snakes and a kid. We found the kid. They killed him. And now they got four women, not just Mrs. Teach. That damned Smallie knew it and he was afraid to keep on after 'em."

This last bit—the part about Smallie being afraid— Hobie fairly spat out.

Garner was not surprised about Smallie, but said, "Four women?" The last he'd heard, Mrs. Teach was the only hostage. This put a whole different slant on things.

Hobie nodded emphatically. "Yessir. A mother and a daughter that they took from a ranch somewhere outside Silverbell, and a soiled dove that they snatched right here in Bisbee."

Garner thumbed back his hat and scratched his chin before he said, "Aw, shit."

In a tone that stopped just short of pleading, Hobie added, "Boss, the Lowell girl—the daughter, I mean—is only fourteen."

Well, that did it. Garner stood up, then looked down at

Hobie. "Well, what you sitting around for? There are still a good two and a half hours of daylight left."

Suddenly beaming, Hobie leapt up, grabbed his saddle-bags and bedroll, and beat Garner to the door.

Ike Smeed and Milt Chambers rode into Galgo a little after sunset, leading a string of three horses—and three weary women with little hope—behind them. Mary Teach was last in the line.

The town of Galgo was nothing special, she thought as her horse plodded down the center of the street. Dusty adobes lined in rows, the line broken occasionally by a clapboard building or a rough shed or a modest stone structure. The clapboards were mostly places of business. All the signs were in Spanish, but she managed to identify a mercantile and a dry-goods store by the activity and the barrels out front, and a livery stable by the smell.

A few people wandered along the streets. A little man in an ill-fitting uniform of sorts went down the row, stopping every half block to light the gas jets that lit the street. Mary was surprised to see those, but she reminded herself that Galgo was a coastal town and a port of sorts—or at least, it had been—and would therefore have a few more fineries than a remote village.

It wasn't much bigger, though. The little man lighting the gaslights along the main street only had to ignite seven jets before he came to the end and crossed to the other side.

And the people were rather queer, she noted. Either peasants, dressed in simple garb, usually sun-bleached cotton, or south-of-the-border dandies. It was either brocade or plain cotton, no in-between. Some of the men in brocade stopped to study the women as they rode along.

But not a soul seemed to think it odd that three women who had obviously been mistreated, three women whose hands were bound and whose clothing was in tatters, were being led down the center of the main street.

Becky Lowell, on the horse ahead, turned her head back and forth, and Mary could tell she was growing increasingly distraught. Mary opened her mouth to say something to the girl, some words of comfort that she hadn't quite formed yet, when Becky cried out, "Help us! Help us, please! Can't you see we've been kidnapped?"

And the men to whom she had called out, both brocade dandies, laughed. Laughed, and then went inside the building they were smoking in front of.

And that was when Mary knew they were doomed. That laughter sealed it.

Milt Chambers had reined in his horse immediately, and when Becky came up next to him, he slapped her across the face and cursed her. "Shut up, you little bitch," he snarled before he rode ahead again.

To the sound of Becky's weeping, they at last came to a halt beyond the gaslights and dismounted before a large stone building. Mary went to Becky immediately and took Becky's bound hands in hers.

"It's all right, child," she soothed. "Be strong."

"What does it matter?" Becky wept as Ike Smeed roughly grabbed her shoulder and shoved her toward the door.

9

"She's never going to be right again, is she?" Becky asked
softly. They were inside the old stone building, locked in
a spiderwebbed, windowless cell, and the only light was
a soft flicker from the torch outside in the corridor. It
must have been built by long-ago explorers or Spanish
conquistadors, Mary thought. They had made slaves of
the Indians, hadn't they?

This was surely a prison. All the walls were solid
stone, save for the rusting bars of the door and its massive lock, but Mary could hear faint weeping coming
from down the corridor they'd been led along. They were
not alone.

Mary glanced over at Agatha, covered in a crude serape that Smeed had tossed over her before they rode into
town. Not to hide her nakedness, Mary decided. To hide
the scrapes and bruises and peeling, sunburnt skin that
covered her torso.

Agatha sat, her back against the wall, her legs artlessly
splayed in front of her on the floor, staring straight ahead.

She was still mute, still appeared not to hear anything said to her.

Poor Agatha. Poor Becky.

The women's bonds had been removed just before Chambers and Smeed left, voicing their intentions to go the local cantina and tie one on, so Mary was able to put her arms around Becky's shoulders.

"I don't know, sweetie," she whispered, and hugged Becky close. "Maybe she's better off. Not knowing, I mean."

"I miss her," Becky said softly. "I miss her so much." She reached out and put a hand on her mother's arm. It had no effect on Agatha. After a moment, Becky pulled back rather abruptly, as if she'd just touched something alien. "She's not in there anymore," she said, her hand trembling. "It's like she's gone off somewhere."

Mary, at a loss for words, slowly stood up and went to the tiny cell's door. The weeping that had drifted toward her earlier had stopped, but she called out, "Is anyone there?"

After a pause, a voice answered her. A soft voice, a young voice. "H-hello?" It was more a breathed word than a spoken one.

Mary closed her eyes for a moment, torn between joy that they were not alone, and sorrow that there were others about to share their fate. "My name's Mary Teach," she said.

"Nancy," came the answer to Mary's unspoken question. "Nancy Bullock. Can you help me? Please?"

"We're locked in, the same as you," Mary answered. At least, she assumed the girl was locked in another cell. "Do you know what they're going to do with us?"

"Sell us," the girl said with a sad sort of resigned hopelessness in her voice. "Sell us to the highest bidder, I reckon. I was gonna get married next month. I was

gonna marry Tommy Wheeler and we were gonna go up
to Oregon. His uncle has a place there."

"What happened?" Mary whispered. She was almost
afraid to ask.

Nancy sighed, then said, "Mexican bandits came on
our ranch. They took me. They killed Ma and Papa. I
don't know about my little brother. They said they were
taking me to the auction. They said I'd bring a pretty
price, being as I was a virgin." Halfway through this confession, poor Nancy had begun to weep again.

A new voice joined in, this one older and harder.
"Mary? My name's Flo Heckert."

Mary said, "Hello, Flo." Beside her, Becky rose and
came to the cell door, too. "I'm here with Becky and
Agatha Lowell."

"You gals from Arizona or California, or someplace
south of the border?" Flo asked.

"Arizona, ma'am," Becky offered.

Flo's voice, a little like a crosscut saw going through
green wood, replied, "Well, me and Pansy, here, we
worked at a place on the border, at Nogales. Goddamn
kidnappin' swine come in the night and bundled us off.
We'd seen 'em before, the bastards. They come in about
a week before to check out the new gals."

Becky whispered, "Does she mean they were soiled
doves? Like Nellie was?"

"Shh," Mary hissed softly.

"I am Juanita," said a silky voice with a thick Spanish
accent. "I am seventeen. They took me at night, from my
father's house."

"Maria Alba, from El Paso," said another Spanish
voice.

"I'm Joan," whispered a new voice.

"I'm Tansy," said another.

"I am Elena."

"Bethie Simmons."

The voices went on and on and on, each more pitiful and lost than the last, and soon Mary realized there were more then twenty women in this place, more than twenty captives. And then, from beside her, Becky asked, "What are they going to do with us? Was that lady right?"

Mary's heart was too heavy to answer, but Florence's wasn't.

"Sell us," Flo spat. "Wasn't you listenin'? They're gonna sell us like cattle on the auction block."

Becky paled while the unseen Florence continued. "There's men here from all over. South America, mostly. This here's a white slave market, honey. The 'ladies only' kind. They're gonna auction us to the highest bidders, and after, we'll set sail in one'a them tall ships down at the harbor and end up in God knows where. Peru, maybe, or Bolivia."

Soft weeping from down the corridor sent chilly fingers up Mary's spine, and she hugged Becky's shoulders a little tighter. She'd never heard anyone say it out loud, say it so matter-of-factly. One of the Spanish women, Mary didn't know who, wailed, *"Dios Mio,"* and began to cry loudly.

Becky began to weep, too, but silently, hopelessly. "Mary," she whispered. "Oh, Mary, what will we do?"

Flo had pretty good ears because, from down the row, she replied, "Get used to the idea, honey."

In town, at the nearest cantina, Ike Smeed and Milt Chambers were celebrating. It was premature, perhaps, but at least they had the women safely delivered to the auction.

Well, three of them, anyway.

Chambers lolled back in his chair, one hand gripping his beer mug, one foot on the scarred table. The more he drank the madder he got about that Nellie, all over again.

"Damn stupid, Ike," he repeated drunkenly. "Goddamn stupid."

"Quit sayin' that!" Smeed growled. He was well into his cups, too. They'd had a few shots of tequila before settling down to mugs of warm Mexican beer, and they were on their third round of that. "I already said I was sorry about two hundred times. And you would'a done the same, Chambers."

Chambers shrugged. "Maybe, maybe not. Point is, you was the one that done it. Probably done us out of six or eight hundred, easy."

"That's a load'a horseshit," Smeed replied crankily. He tossed back the last of his beer, then waved at the bartender and held up two fingers. *"Dos cervezas!"* He turned back toward Chambers and growled, "Two hundred, tops. Ain't nobody gonna pay for a dove. Not much, anyhow."

The bartender slid two fresh beers onto the table. The beer was like pony piss, but it was handy.

Smeed waited until the bartender left, then leaned across the table. "You would'a done just the same and you know it," he hissed, four inches away from Chambers's face.

Chambers picked up the new beer and leaned back. "Ike?" he said. "Don't you ever brush your teeth?"

The next morning, Garner and Hobie picked up the trail. The boys they were following hadn't bothered to hide it, but time and the wind had softened their tracks quite a bit. Still, there were places where Garner was able to follow at a lope. Most of the rest of the time, he kept an eye on the trail from a soft jog.

He was riding Faro, having left Pepper in Bisbee to heal up. Hobie had rented a good-natured fifteen-hand bay mule from the stable where Pepper was boarded, and led it behind Fly. The mule was packed with all their foodstuffs and possibles.

The terrain was sere, the surrounding area devoid of any life save for the occasional coyote or jackrabbit or circling hawk. Even Hobie had given up on talking, which was pretty unusual for him, especially this early in the day.

Garner didn't mind, though. He had his nose to the scent like a bloodhound, and had little time for anything else. He was pleased that they were making such good time, too. While the men they were tracking had traveled at a walk or a jog, he and Hobie were able to move much faster. They were already across the border and into Mexico, traveling over what was near to a desert.

Garner loped around cactus, leading Hobie a merry trail to follow with that mule. No words of complaint, though. And Garner was actually enjoying this. He was out of the country and he was completely unofficial. He knew damned well that his deputy U.S. marshal's badge didn't mean squat down here, and he'd stuck it in his back pocket, out of sight, out of mind.

It was just as well. Having no strings had a price, and if not using that badge was the price he had to pay for being shed of the responsibility of keeping to the straight and narrow and reporting in to Holling Eberhart—or far worse, Ned Smallie—then so be it.

And then he rode around a hummock of manzanita. He whoaed Faro abruptly, and Hobie and Fly just about crashed into him. As it was, the mule broke loose and cantered ahead about twenty feet before it stopped and look back at them.

"Aw, crud," said Hobie. Garner didn't figure he was talking about the mule.

While Hobie clucked to Fly and rode ahead to grab the mule's rope again, Garner dismounted. He ground-tied Faro and walked toward the site of a camp. And then he walked past it, to a place where manzanita had been pulled up and piled high over something the buzzards were picking at and fighting over.

With a wave of his hat, he shooed away most of the birds, and kicked at enough manzanita to see what they'd been feasting on.

"Sonofabitch," he cursed.

Hobie, at his side by this time, echoed his words. Thick-voiced, he asked, "You . . . you reckon she's Mrs. Teach?"

Garner shook his head. "She's not dressed like any ranch wife I've ever seen." He sighed and thumbed back his hat. "I guess she's likely the saloon gal they picked up in Bisbee. Those boys circled all over hell and gone!"

"Tell me about it," said Hobie. "I was the one foll'in' 'em with that darned posse."

Garner grunted, then said, "Pull the shovel from the pack, Hobie. We haven't got time to do much for her, but at least we can give her a little dirt."

Sam Teach and Will Thurlow were not far away. In fact, if Hobie had stood up on his saddle and scouted the surrounding territory, he could have seen them: two specks heading slowly south.

Will was well past being concerned about the Captain. He let Teach ride ahead of him so that he could keep watch over the man without being obvious. It was only ten o'clock, and Teach was already swaying in the saddle. Will didn't think it was too much laudanum. He still controlled it, and had let the Captain have only what he considered a proper dose. Not too much, not too little. But the Captain was swaying nonetheless.

Will took a chance on getting his head bitten off, and rode up even with the Captain. "Captain Teach?" he said.

Through gritted teeth, Teach replied, "You're awful damn formal today."

Will couldn't help but smile a little. "Sorry," he said. "Why don't we take a rest? The horses are about ready."

This last part was a lie, for the horses hadn't been moving faster than a plod all morning, and they had started out late to boot. But he figured it was better to lie than to point out that the Captain looked as if he was going to haul off and keel straight over at any given moment.

Teach didn't fight him on it or call him on his fib. In fact, he reined in his horse and said, "Sounds like a fine idea, Will."

Will supposed that the Captain meant it to come out light and jovial, but his voice sounded exhausted. *This is going to end bad,* Will thought as he led the horses into the meager patch of pale shade offered by a prickly pear. *Bad for everybody concerned.*

He tethered the horses, then watered them, all the time stealing quick glances at his companion, who had taken refuge in the pool of shade cast by a low boulder. Captain Teach looked even worse on the ground than he had in the saddle. Pain lined his face and tortured what few halting movements he made.

Will hadn't looked to see him dismount. The Captain wouldn't have wanted him to.

Will pulled down his canteen and joined the Captain in the shade. Well, part of him did. When he sat down, his legs jutted out in the baking sun.

He opened his canteen and took a swig. It was warm, but it was welcome.

He said, "Captain? You reckon you could use another swig of laudanum?"

Teach turned toward him, and beneath the tan, his face was pale with pain. "I suppose it wouldn't hurt, Will," he said.

Trying to appear unworried, Will reached into his

pocket and fished for the bottle. "Where's it paining you? In your lungs or in your back?"

"Back," Teach replied stiffly. "Lung hasn't bothered me in a while."

Will handed him the bottle and watched him take a short sip, study on it for a moment, then take another. He handed the bottle back. "That should do me for a while," he said.

Will corked, then pocketed the bottle. Maybe that was the trouble. He just hadn't given the Captain quite enough this morning. It was awful hard to tell how much was right.

He decided that they'd just sit there for a while, just sit there until the medicine had a chance to take hold real good and the Captain was feeling better.

"Why don't you just lean back for a spell, Captain?" he said. "I'd like to give the horses a good breather. I'm tired, too."

The Captain pulled his hat down over his eyes and said, "You always were a terrible liar, Will."

"Yes, sir, was and am."

"You're a damned good friend, though."

Will didn't answer.

10

At about four that afternoon, while the Captain and Will were stopped once again, riders came into sight.

The Captain didn't see them. He'd just had another couple of doses of laudanum, and was drowsing. And Will thought that this was a fine time to have company, yes, sir, a goddamn wonderful time.

He slid his rifle from its boot and took poor cover behind a clump at grass, the tallest vegetation for about twenty feet in any direction, and waited.

He didn't think they were bandits. That had been his first thought. After all, who else would be crazy enough to be out here? But after a few minutes, he decided against that theory. There were only two of them, leading a packhorse or a mule. Still too far to tell. And they weren't exactly headed straight for him and the Captain. But they sure were traveling at a fast rate.

And then they reined in. One of them pointed at Shorty and Butter Pie. They sat there for a few minutes, like they were talking over what to do, and then they changed their direction a mite and started right toward Will.

Will waited, flat on his stomach, until they rode close enough that he could see that they were American. That was a blessing. At least he and the Captain wouldn't die at the hands of *bandidos*. And then he noticed that when the one on the buckskin moved, something shiny glinted on his shirt, beneath his flapping vest.

Will relaxed, but not much. "Aw, shit," he mumbled as he got to his feet. "Ned Smallie and his bunch."

And then he got to wondering why Smallie was down south of the border, and what the hell Smallie was doing on this case again, a case he'd given up days ago.

Will didn't have long to wonder. Neither of the riders was Ned Smallie.

They stopped about ten yards out from where Will stood, his rifle still in his hands and pointed toward them. "Who goes there?" he barked in his best sergeant's voice.

The older one held his hands wide and empty, and said, "King Garner. My friend, here, is Hobie Hobson. Just headed down to Galgo to see about some horses."

Will pondered this for a second. These two didn't fit the description of the men he and the Captain were looking for. And besides, they'd been going the wrong direction in a pretty big hurry.

"Come on in," he hollered, and let the rifle swing down in his hand. "Can't offer you any shade."

"Who's that?" slurred the Captain, who had momentarily regained some sensibility and clumsily propped himself up on one elbow. Will was certain he'd given the Captain too much medicine this time. Or rather, that the Captain had gulped too much before he'd gotten the bottle away from him.

"Riders," Will replied. "Somebody Garner and Hobie Somebody." His eyes were on the riders, though.

The Captain sagged back down into a recline. "Garner," he breathed, his eyes closing. "Used to know an old brush-popper named Garner."

Before Will could ask him just where he knew this Garner from—if, indeed, it was the same Garner—the riders were in camp. The youngest dismounted first and came forward, his hand out. "Howdy," the boy said. "Hobie Hobson."

Will switched the rifle to his left hand and clasped Hobie's narrow hand in his. "Will Thurlow," he said. He watched as the bigger man, old enough to be the boy's father, got down off his bay.

He offered his hand to Will, too, all the while looking him up and down. "King Garner," he said. "What're you doing down in Mexico, Mr. Thurlow?"

Hobie had discovered the Captain by this time, and before Will could reply, he said, "Hey, is this feller all right?"

"He's sleepin'," Will replied in a tone that said he'd brook no further questions. And then he turned toward Garner again. "I don't believe I ever heard of anybody goin' to Galgo for horses, Mr. Garner. Cattle, yes. But horses, no."

Garner didn't back down an inch. He set his jaw and said, "First time for everything, I reckon. You didn't answer my question."

Will, too, straightened up a little taller. "We're looking for somebody. Somebody who got . . . lost. And if you're a mind to start any trouble, Garner—"

"Whoa, whoa, whoa!" said Hobie, and stepped between them. "You fellers want to calm down? Boss, this man over here says his name's Sam Teach."

Garner's eyes narrowed. "Teach?"

Hobie nodded.

Will looked toward the Captain. His eyes were half-lidded, and Will supposed he could have roused enough to tell the boy his name.

"One and the same," said Hobie.

"I believe we're on the same side of this, Thurlow," Garner said, after a long sigh. "We're tracking your friend's wife and the bastards that kidnapped her."

Will felt himself sag with relief, but he asked Hobie, "That a badge under there?"

Hobie held his vest aside for a moment, displaying the silver of a deputy U.S. marshal's badge. "We're not quite official down here," he confided. "And the boss's got one, too, except he hardly ever wears it."

"Hobie?" said Garner.

"Yeah, Boss?"

"The horses."

"Yeah, Boss."

As the boy trudged off, leading their horses and their mule toward the picket line where Will had staked his and the Captain's mounts, Garner said, "I'll be damned. Would that be Lieutenant Teach?"

This gave Will a little bit of a start, but he said, "Major Teach. Retired. I was his sergeant."

Garner studied on this for a second, then asked, "What's really the matter with him? He looks like shit warmed over."

No one bothered the women all night and all day. No one brought them water, either, or food. But round about five in the evening—a fact that was borne out by the pocket watch that one of the women down the corridor carried—two men opened the outside doors.

The dim light was so sudden that it stabbed at Mary's eyes. Becky blinked and winced, too. Agatha was slumped too far inside the cell to notice, even if she had been lucid.

With an echo of boots on stone, they walked toward

the shadows of Mary's cell door, then far past it. She heard the women's pleas of *"¡Agua, por favor!"* and "Water!" but the men did not reply.

Instead, she heard the clink of keys, then somebody's wails of "No-no-no!" There were quick, gruff words in Spanish, then the pop of a fist on flesh, and then quiet. A few moments later the two men came back up the hallway, dragging an unconscious woman between them. The toes of her shoes made a sad little *click-scuff-click* on the paving stones of the floor as they dragged her past, and then outside.

A moment later, one of the men stepped back inside the structure and shouted something in Spanish, then gestured, as if he wanted someone to translate. One of the Spanish women obliged and called, "He says not to make any trouble. He says they are taking us from this place."

"Where?" Becky whispered. The girl was practically plastered to Mary's side.

"I don't know, honey," Mary said softly. The man proceeded down the corridor, and again they heard the distant clanking of keys. Mary pulled Becky closer and peered over her shoulder at the mute Agatha. "I don't know."

"You take good care of your horses," Garner said. It was just coming sunset, and the men had decided to camp where Will and Teach had stopped. Teach was in no condition to travel, Garner had quickly ascertained. He had probed Will Thurlow for the details, and had been almost sorry that he had. It was a hell of a story.

Garner patted Faro's neck.

Will grinned, and put Butter Pie's nose bag back in his pack. "I try to," he answered. "Man's no good afoot in country like this. And they're peaceable critters, ain't they?"

"That they are," Garner said. He had taken a liking to Will Thurlow. He hoped that Sam Teach appreciated what a good friend he had in this man.

Hobie had managed to gather enough wood for a fire and enough twigs to kindle it, and was busily arranging them when Garner and Will walked back from the horses.

"There's not enough to keep goin' all night, but enough to get the coffee good and hot and get us some dinner fried," Hobie said in response to Garner's unspoken question.

Garner grunted. "How you doin', Teach? You awake enough to remember me, yet?"

Teach opened his eyes and squinted. "I remembered you right away, Garner," he said right out. Garner thought he put words together pretty well for a man who was as soaked in laudanum as Will had indicated he was. "It's been a while."

Garner sat down on his heels and proceeded to roll himself a cigarette. "That it has," he said.

"That Apache buck," said Teach. "Did he leave you with a scar?"

Garner snorted. "Right along my ribs. Bad aim."

Teach smiled a bit. "I'm guessing it would take quite a bit more than that to kill you, Garner."

"What Apache was that?" said Will. "Captain, I don't recall any time we fought Apache that this feller was—"

"Before," said Teach, and sagged back. He seemed to have shot his conversational wad for the time being.

But Hobie sure hadn't. "Before what?" he asked eagerly.

"Guess he means before he got to the fort," Garner said.

"And?" insisted Will.

Garner shrugged and lit his smoke. "I was down south,

along the old Ox Bow route. This was in the early seventies."

"Seventy-five," corrected Teach from behind closed eyes.

"Whatever," Garner continued curtly. "Anyway, I saw this little band of shiny new troopers pinned down by a war party. Another band of reservation-jumpers. So I got rid of the Apache." He shrugged. "That was all."

"What do you mean, 'That was all'?" Hobie cried indignantly. "I never read that in any of the books!"

Garner whipped toward him. "I knew it! You been reading those stupid books again."

The startled kid turned white as milk. "I—I—"

"I know where you've got those books hid, Hobie," Garner said angrily, and then took pity on the boy. After all, he'd found those dime novels a good six months ago. It looked like they'd been read to pieces, too. He hadn't come down on the boy then. Why should he now?

"I told you, Hobie," he went on, more gently this time, "don't believe 'em. They're half lies, and even the parts that are true aren't exactly true. I would have thought that getting yourself written up by that No-Ears Clive Woolsey would've taught you a lesson."

"'Scuse me," said Will, shaking his head disapprovingly. "You want to go back to the part where you got rid of the damned Apaches?" He gave his head a shake. "I'm sorry, Garner, but I mean, one man . . ."

"He did it," croaked Sam Teach, who seemed to have gotten himself a second wind. "We heard somebody holler, 'Sound the charge, you blue-coated fools!' And when MacGarrity blew a lungful of wind into that bugle, well, it all of a sudden sounded like every gun in the world was up in the rocks. We opened up with everything we had left—which wasn't much—and I'll be damned if those Apache didn't turn tail."

Garner nodded his head.

Teach added, "Course, Garner had to try and jump one of them when he was hightailing it."

"Well, the stupid sonofabitch rode right under the rock I was perched on," Garner interjected.

"And Garner took his spear along the ribs," continued Teach, although Garner could tell he was growing weak again. "We tried to talk him into going to the fort with us, but he wouldn't have any of it. We ended by just patching him up and letting him go his way."

Softly, Will said, "You never told me any of that, Captain."

If there was a reproach in there anywhere, Garner didn't hear it.

"Sorry, Will," Teach said with a faint hint of a smile. He closed his eyes. "By the time you got assigned to me, we were too busy fighting Apache of our own."

Will hoisted a brow and sat back. "That we were, Captain, that we were."

"Will?" said Hobie quietly. "I believe he's dozed off again."

"Well, we'll wake him in time for supper," Garner said, and stubbed out his smoke. "What you got in mind to whip together, Hobie?"

The women were placed in two wagons that were barred all around with iron and padlocked at the rear. There were twenty-two of them altogether, eleven in each wagon. Mary had counted twice. She sat on the sawdust bed of the conveyance between Agatha, who had come along peaceably enough, and Becky, who trembled uncontrollably.

Mary couldn't thing of a thing to calm the child. She was shaking just as hard.

It was getting dark, and she was thirsty, so thirsty. As if one of the men had read her mind, he appeared with a bucket and a dipper, and stood mutely alongside the wagon while the dehydrated women scrambled for a turn.

At last, with a jerk and a lurch, the rattling wagons pulled out. In the dimming light, they started down the dusty road that led out of town.

11

After a jolting ride that lasted only long enough for the sun to go down, the wagons turned from a dark, bumpy, desert road and started down a long and winding lane, set off from the desert by a line of tall cypress trees on either side. Mary pulled herself from Becky's grip and stood, balancing herself by clinging to the bars that surrounded them.

Soon she made out their destination: a distant, vast, and ominous hacienda. Windows glowed like eyes and shadows loomed, even though an attempt had been made to light it with rows of smoking torches on the lawn. It stood alone, high on the crest of a hill. Or perhaps it was a cliff. She thought she could hear the sea as if from far away, hear it crashing.

Again she was overtaken by a fierce shaking, one that came not from the rattling, shifting floor of the wagon, but from deep inside her.

Unconsciously, she rested a hand on her belly, as if to comfort and protect her unborn child.

The wagons pulled up at the far end of the hacienda,

which was even larger than she'd imagined when she'd first seen it. She wondered why they were being taken to a place like this. And then she wondered why she had questioned it at all. She had no experience in these matters. Why should she? She should have learned by this time to be surprised at nothing.

And then, while the other wagon was being unloaded and the women from it being led off, she thought of what Sam had said about Señor Carlos Ruiz Lopez's house. She remembered him before she left, telling her all about Señor Lopez's hacienda as if he'd been there already, already sold the bull.

"Sam Teach, you oughtn't take everything Bill Bundy says to heart," she had teased him on the night before he left.

"But he knows, Mary," Sam had said with a grin, and took another plate from her to wipe dry. "He's been there in person. Bought himself a few head of half-bred Brahman cows a couple years back. Said it's practically a palace. Right on the seacoast and everything."

"Well," she'd replied, sudsing another dish, "sometimes Bill Bundy's so deep in his cups that he thinks the whole world's a palace. Just don't be disappointed, that's all."

And he'd hugged her tight and said, "Honey, don't you know that my whole world's a palace when I'm coming home to you?" And he'd put his hand on her belly and kissed her temple.

Mary's eyes brimmed with unspent tears as a rough-looking man unlocked the door of the wagon and gestured at them to hurry. Armed guards, two of them, stood behind him with rifles.

As if we'd know where to run, Mary thought despondently as she motioned to Becky. "Help your mother, dear," she said in a whisper, and hopped to the ground.

Propping Agatha between them, Mary and Becky followed the women in front of them toward the side of the hacienda, and once again, Mary thought of Sam's description. Funny, but she'd always pictured Mexico as a land filled with nothing outside of Mexico City but peasants and hovels. Now she was wondering if every other person down here owned a castle, or the Mexican equivalent of one.

And it wasn't until they had walked to a small door and a mustachioed, swarthy fellow poked her with his rifle and said something that sounded like "Move!" that she realized that she'd almost given up.

Mary paused to square her shoulders and take a deep breath. And the guard poked her in the back again.

She whirled toward him and slapped the rifle barrel away.

He stood there a moment, blinking with surprise, and then the other guard laughed and said something in Spanish. She didn't wait to see the first guard's reaction. She turned on her heel and walked inside, holding her head high. They might have her body, but they'd never have her spirit.

And Sam would come. He would be coming any second now.

Sam Teach drowsed beside the campfire. He had stood up—or at least, he thought he had—earlier in the evening and taken some steps, and said something about getting their sorry asses on their horses. Demanded it, actually. And then Will had given him some more of that poppy juice, and pretty soon he'd calmed down, all right. He'd calmed down so much that he knew he was beside a campfire, but couldn't always figure which one it was. Or *when* it was.

At the moment, he figured that Will and those two new fellows were out there. Hobie and Garner, right? He was awfully glad they'd bumped into Garner. Good man in a fight. Or at least, he used to be.

Of course, maybe it wasn't Garner at all. Maybe he'd made the whole thing up in his head. A gift of the laudanum. Maybe he was still back in Will and Bess's spare room.

But he thought not. His eyes were closed, the lids so heavy that he couldn't raise them, not even for a tiny, slitted peep, but he could hear voices. Several of them. And he thought that Will had said, "Garner," several times. And the ground was far too hard to be a down mattress.

He drifted away from his body and the fire and the voices, and began to think about Mary again. As if she wasn't on his mind constantly, as if the absence of her presence wasn't like a jagged chink taken out of his own soul. Mary, with the robin's-egg eyes; Mary, with the quick laugh; Mary, oh, Mary . . .

Fitfully, he drifted off to sleep.

The women were pushed into a large, windowless room, devoid of furniture and lit by torches. There was a small stage-like platform at one end. After everyone was in, guards included, someone closed the door. Mary heard the latch lock firmly behind them. And then two men stepped out onto the platform, men she'd never seen before.

"Welcome, ladies," said the first man. He was big and tall, and not ugly, unless you counted what he was doing.

The second repeated the greeting in Spanish.

"You will be allowed to clean yourselves," the man continued, with the second one echoing his words in Spanish, "and wash your hair. Clean clothes will be provided for you. You will be served supper."

"And then what?" asked a voice. Mary couldn't see, but she thought it belonged to Flo, the soiled dove from Nogales.

"And then you will attend a little gathering. In your honor," said the man, a slight smirk on his face. "Make sure you all look pretty." He waited for his friend to finish the translation, and then they both turned on their heels and exited the way they'd come.

"In a pig's eye," muttered the unseen Flo.

Which set off a buzzing hum of conversation. Mary didn't join in, though. Her knees felt suddenly weak, as if they were made of aspic, and she wobbled a little, catching herself on Becky's shoulder.

Becky, who was busy holding her mother up, turned toward Mary and whispered, "What do they mean, look pretty? What's happening, Mary?"

Before Mary had a chance to answer, one of the guards shouted, *"¡Silencio!"* and the others began herding them toward a side door.

Weak-kneed, Mary was pushed along in the throng, and funneled through the doorway. She emerged in a second room, this one lit by hanging lanterns and lined with six bathtubs filled with steaming, fragrant water. Roughly half of the women were pushed on, into the next room, and then the door between them was closed.

At this point, the male guards disappeared, and the women were left alone.

After a long moment of silence, one of the women suddenly cried, "Me first!" ripped off her clothes, and leapt into one of the tubs, splashing water over every woman in a ten-foot radius.

Becky turned toward Mary. "It's a bath," she shrugged. "It'll wash off those . . . those . . ."

"I know," Mary said. She, too, wanted to wash away every vestige of Ike Smeed and Milt Chambers's touch. In fact, she wished they were here right now. She'd drown them in one of those tubs. Looking around at these women—all filthy, all scared, some trembling, and mostly mad as hell—she was fairly certain she'd have plenty of help.

"Let's see to your mother first, all right?" she said.

"Yes, ma'am," Becky said, and dragged her mother toward the nearest tub. "This ones's ours," she announced to the room, staking their claim.

Sometime while Agatha was dully, mindlessly going through the motions of bathing, sometime when both Mary and Becky turned their heads, one moment when they failed to pay attention, Agatha silently slipped beneath the water and drowned.

There was nothing to be done, and it happened fast, so very fast.

"Help me! Help me!" Mary cried to Becky, and Becky dropped the dresses she'd been going through. Several women rushed to Mary's side. Several helped pull Agatha from the water.

But it was too late.

"Never heard of anybody drowning so damned fast," said one of the others, shaking her head sadly.

"Wish I could," muttered another. "Wish I had the courage."

Courage had nothing to do with it, thought Mary as she comforted the sobbing Becky. Agatha had died days ago, the moment Smeed and Chambers had ridden onto her ranch. This just made it official.

Numbly, Becky and Mary bathed, albeit in another tub. The water was still warm and fragrant, despite the filthy women who had used it before her, and Mary almost smiled. It felt so comforting, so womblike, especially after all she had been through. The scent of lilacs tickled her nose, both from the salts in the water and the soap, which wasn't the lye soap that she had expected. It was fancy, made up in little molds in the form of some sort of crest.

She lathered herself generously, grateful for anything resembling civilization.

And the clothes that had been provided for them? Mary didn't understand it. They were wonderful clothes, beautiful things. Even poor Agatha benefited. They dried her and clothed her in a soft pink dress, then reverently laid her out on a bench. Her face was relaxed in death, and the dress hid most of the bruises and cuts she'd suffered. She looked the closest to peace that Mary had seen her.

Becky, who was sniffling as she tried to brush her dead mother's hair dry, had donned a crisp new frock the color of celery.

Mary had picked out a pale mustard-colored dress, trimmed in deeper yellow, and it lay waiting for her. It wasn't the best color for her, but then, she wasn't at all certain that she wanted to look her best.

It was doubtful that she would, anyhow. Or that Becky would, either. The both of them were still covered with scrapes and bruises.

It was a sorry thing to admit, but Mary half-envied Agatha.

A door opened, and the few women still in the tubs pulled washcloths or towels up to their chins. But no one came in. A voice announced, "Fifteen minutes until dinner, ladies," repeated it in Spanish, and then the door closed again.

"You'd best hurry, Mary," called an expressionless Becky.

Her hair still damp against her neck, but the mustard-yellow dress cloaking most of her bruises, Mary dragged Becky along behind her in the line. By twos, the women walked up an interior circular staircase that was encased on all sides by a stucco wall. At last they gained the top and spread out on the landing. Mary, being toward the back of the group, had a chance to peek out the barred window.

Two stories below, the front of the hacienda was much changed. There were buggies and broughams and coaches now, lined up in rows between the torches. Drivers lounged against the hitching rails or the sides of the buggies, and some were drinking. A Mexican woman passed dolefully among them, carrying a tray with more beer mugs.

Men wealthy enough to afford coaches and drivers were here, and they were here in great number.

And they were here, she realized with a shudder, to bid on herself and her hapless companions.

Even those who hadn't had a chance to look outside sensed the situation. A hush, broken only by Becky's soft whimpering, fell over them, and then the door opened.

Music flooded out, gay music, happy music, but nary a smile touched the women's lips.

The man who had spoken to them before stepped forward and said something in Spanish, and then repeated it in English. He said, "I doubt there is one among you who does not know the reason she has been brought here."

Becky sniffled, and Mary hugged her tighter.

The man paused for a moment, and took a long look around him at the surrounding sea of women. "Be encouraged that you will have a life of adventure," he began again at last. "But be aware that you must live a life of obedience, as well. The men who are here to purchase you are wealthy and powerful. This is the end of your old life, and the beginning of the new. No one will save you. No one will come for you. And if you are not fetching and coquettish tonight, no one will buy you."

He paused for a moment, then continued. "And we cannot have that. *You* cannot have that. Do you understand?"

Becky whispered, "Mary?"

Quietly, Mary said, "I believe he's telling us that if we don't bamboozle somebody into buying us, we're as good as dead."

Just as Becky slapped a hand over her own mouth to keep from shrieking, the man, who had much better ears than Mary could have expected, said, "You judge the situation correctly, madam."

He stepped aside, and the women were ushered through the door and onto a wide balcony.

Mary didn't know what she had expected, but what she saw once she had gone through the doorway was not it.

Lively music welled from below, and the smells of roasting meats and rich sauces overtook Mary's starved senses. There also came to her a wave of noise, of laughter, of voices, of clanking silver and colliding earthenware: a party in progress, and a big one.

In the large, open courtyard, servants passed through clusters of revelers, who sat in groups of four or five or six at large, fancifully carved wooden tables. These were laden with steaming bowls and platters of food, polished silver candelabras, wine bottles, golden and silver goblets, and luscious flowers. The guests were exclusively male.

They were old, young, and everywhere in between. They lounged in ornately carved chairs with tall backs, and they wore fine Spanish suits. Some stopped their conversations and briefly raised sparkling goblets at the sight of the women. Some glanced up but just kept talking, as if this were an everyday occurrence.

Their faces were ordinary. Just ordinary. Some cruel, some kind, but nothing different than you'd see at a town meeting or a church social. How did men like these, perfectly normal men, come to a place like this, come to buy women?

"Go on," said the man who had spoken to them in the

other room. When none of the women moved, he gave one of them a shove toward the wide, railed staircase. "Go on," he growled. "And remember to be nice. Your very lives depend on it."

"But what about Mama?" Becky whispered as they stumbled toward the stairs. "What about her . . . her body?"

"Hush, child," Mary soothed. "She's past caring or hurting now. She'd want you to take care of yourself."

Although Mary was still putting up a good front, she—who had been so certain all along that her Sam was coming any moment, going to ride in full of blood and thunder and vengeance and save them from this, save them all—was beginning to think that perhaps he wasn't coming. That something terrible had happened to him, for that was, as she saw it, the only thing that could keep him away.

And as she started down the steps toward the milling, laughing, shouting crowd, she felt her heart sink.

12

Across the broad open sweep of the balcony, a knock sounded upon the richly hand-carved door of Señor Carlos Ruiz Lopez's study.

"*¿Sí?*" he said, not bothering to put aside his brandy.

The door opened, and Montoya stuck his head in. "They are ready, *Patrón*," he said in Spanish. "Just coming out onto the plaza now."

Montoya waited a moment, as if he expected Lopez to answer, but when no answer was forthcoming, he bowed his head quickly and ducked back, closing the door behind him.

Lopez still did nothing except slowly swirl his brandy and stare at the end of his cigar, which had gone out perhaps five minutes ago. He would be glad when he was done with this filthy business. At least, glad when it moved next year, to the hacienda of Diego Mondragon, far to the south.

He was not entirely certain how he had come to make this pact so many years ago, couldn't recall the exact conversation or even nodding his head "yes," although he remembered the reason why. But he had decided that this would be the last year for him. He would bow out, let Diego run it himself. He was getting too old to traffic in human flesh. Soon, he thought, he would go to meet his maker, and this was indeed a worrisome thing to have on one's conscience.

It had not been so bad when it started. The girls were bought from families, both Mexican and American, who were so poor that they'd sell their own children for a sack of flour or of beans. Or a small pouch of coins. They were usually ill-educated, if educated at all, and were brought to the stronghold, where they were taught things like manners and cleanliness. Some were even taught to read before going on the auction block.

He had an entirely superior class of buyers, then, too. A few of the good ones, he still had. But he could just imagine the animals eagerly awaiting this year's auction.

It would be better for him if it was far in his past. It would be better if he had a little time to make up for it in the eyes of the Lord.

This year would be the last. He would break it to Diego tonight, after the sale. Diego couldn't blame him, could he? Lopez was ten years his senior, and Diego had been made a rich man from his share of the proceeds. It would more than make up for that small episode that had happened many years ago, the one that Diego had held over his head and that had gotten Lopez in this business of human traffic so long ago. But the one that Diego hadn't mentioned for—what? Perhaps three years now?

Lopez could plead age or family responsibilities, both of which were very true arguments. It was getting more and more difficult to find a reason to send his wife and daughters off to Europe or back to Mexico City for an extended visit at the same time every year, like clockwork. His Constanza, she was getting along, too, and she was wearying of travel, especially travel without him.

Perhaps he could simply move to Europe, back home to Spain.

No, no, that would be too difficult, now that he finally had his cattle herd in something close to order, now that he had at last built his grand hacienda just the way he wanted it, now that his two oldest daughters were married, and married well. Constanza would never leave the country for good, not if it meant leaving Esperanza and Anna behind in this colonial wilderness.

And besides, even if he could coerce Constanza and the other girls to go back to Spain, that little . . . episode . . . would follow him there, too.

It had been a terrible thing for a man to be only thirty-two years old, riding alone—just a little drunk—through a dark street late at night, and be surprised by a fellow lurching out of an alley in his path. A gun was in his hand, and Lopez had been certain the man was going to rob him. He had drawn his pistol and fired without thinking.

It was also a terrible thing that he was such a good shot, a worse thing that the man's weapon had turned out to be nothing more than a silver flask, glinting in the moonlight, and an even worse thing that the man had turned out to be the Spanish ambassador's attaché, exiting from the back door of a house of ill repute.

But that devil Diego Mondragon had been his worst piece of luck that night, for Diego exited only seconds after the Spanish ambassador's attaché did. He heard the shot, saw Lopez crouching over the body, the gun still in his hand, and jumped to the obvious conclusion.

Still, Lopez found meager solace in that Diego was a decidedly dishonest man. He took one look at Lopez's fine clothes and fine mount, and apparently decided that there was more money to be made over the long run than the reward he would receive for turning in a murderer.

And thus had started this "business" of dealing in bought women, stolen women, kidnapped women.

With a sigh, Lopez dropped his cigar into an ashtray, set down his brandy, and stood up. He stepped from behind the desk, gave his embroidered vest a tug to straighten it, then walked to the door.

"The last time," he muttered before he squared his shoulders, turned the latch, and stepped out into the maelstrom.

"And who is this?" said a drunken blond man as he wrapped a meaty hand around Mary's slender waist.

Mary slid free of his grasp, trying to disguise her distaste. After all, Sam was someplace, hurt or delayed. It wouldn't do for him to come for her and find she'd been killed, and all because some filthy pig had put his hands on her. If he came at all.

And then it struck her that this man was an American. She stopped dead in her tracks, suddenly incensed that a fellow American would actually buy people. Had they fought the Civil War for nothing?

"I'm Mary," she snapped. "Please don't grab at me."

The blond cocked an eyebrow and leaned back in his chair, taking her in from head to foot. It was unnerving. It made her feel dirty.

Not as dirty as what Chambers and Smeed had done to her, though, she reminded herself, and then she told herself to be grateful for small favors.

She stood her ground and eyed him back. "Why are you dressed like that?" she asked, referring to his silk brocade vest and short, Spanish jacket. "You're as American as I am."

"Was," he said with a predatory grin. "I'm an Argentino now." He patted his lap. "C'mere, honey."

She didn't move. She said, "And you come here to buy women?"

"If they strike my fancy."

"What for?"

He tipped his head, like a curious vulture. "What'd'ya mean, what for?"

"You're a nice-enough-looking man," Mary said. "You've obviously got money if you came all the way up here. It seems to me that you could get all the women you want for free, back home in Argentina."

He barked out a laugh, then took a long drink from his goblet. "Can't find no American ones, though, honey. Not with your snap. Mary, was it? I'll remember you come bidding time."

With that, he turned his attention away, and Mary was left standing. Not for long, though. A Mexican man, roughly seventy and with a horrible cough, pinched her backside. She whirled around to slap him, but her arm was caught by what she took to be his retainer, a ferret-faced man who wagged his finger and said something in Spanish. The men shared a laugh, then walked away.

The crowd milled around her. She caught a glimpse of several women clinging to walls, hiding their faces, sobbing quietly. And she saw others, too: sinking into men's laps, laughing, sharing their food. She wished she could be as happy about her fate. She searched for Becky, who had been pulled from her side and had disappeared into the crowd the moment they arrived on the main floor. But Becky was nowhere to be seen.

A small Mexican woman, no more than twenty, slipped up beside her, babbled something, and gestured toward the broad banquet table.

"I can't understand you," Mary said. "English?"

"She says you had best eat while you have a chance, Señorita," said a passing fellow in fluent English. He was of moderate height, expensively dressed, and was one of the few who had not stripped her to the skin with his eyes. "I would tend to agree with her," he added before he tipped his hat and moved on.

"This is mad, just mad!" Mary muttered under her breath. "This is Alice through Hell's looking glass!"

And then something strange happened. Something, she instantly realized, that should have happened long ago.

It came to her all in a burst, like champagne that has been shaken and burst its cork.

Sam wasn't coming in time, if at all. "In time" would have been weeks ago, before those filthy pigs laid a hand on her for the first time. She had no one to save her, no one but herself. For the first time in her life she realized this and accepted it. No father, no brother, no husband, no big strong man.

Not even God.

And oddly, her spirits rose, if only a little.

She was alone, except for the child she carried in her belly. And she'd be damned if she'd let them have that tiny life. No, she would live, and her baby would live, but more importantly they would not live as property, as slaves. Of this she was certain.

Smeed and Chambers had killed little coffee-eyed Nellie, who had been braver than all of them put together. At least she had done something, at least she'd had a plan, even if it wasn't a very good one.

All those times that Mary had cooked their dinners and scrubbed their plates, all those times when she had been free to move about the camp . . . Why hadn't she simply used that little knife on Smeed and Chambers, the knife she'd stolen for Nellie? Why hadn't she cracked them over their heads with their own iron skillet, thrown hot grease in their faces, something, anything?

There were a legion of reasons, a whole raft of excuses that sped through her mind too quickly to catch, but she got the gist of them. Oh, she got the gist, all right, and in the time it took to turn around.

There was Becky, now visible as she clung to the end of the buffet table like a pale, pale bird.

Mary started toward her, only to by stopped by a large hand, planted on her stomach. She shoved it away.

The man to whom the hand belonged, a prosperous-looking Mexican, growled something at her in Spanish, then shook his fist.

She shook her fist right back at him, and he was startled enough that she was able to stride past him, her heart pounding a mile a minute, and walk through the crowd to Becky.

Hugging the girl beneath her arm, she stood erect and cried, "Does anyone here speak English?"

One of the Mexican guards stationed at the doors barked at her in Spanish, probably telling her to close her mouth and be a good little girl, a good little slave, but she called again, "I said, does anyone here speak any English?"

Several men moved forward, the looks on their faces ranging from irritation to amusement. Mary turned toward the friendliest looking one, if any men in these circumstances could be termed friendly.

Without preamble, she said, "This girl's mother has died tonight, and she's beside herself with grief. She needs to mourn. I demand that we be taken to a private room."

Just like that, the entire room fell silent.

Mary didn't back down, though. She stood her ground bravely, pulling the silently weeping Becky close.

The man to whom she had addressed this speech, the one who had looked at least partially pleasant, said nothing, though. Instead, he was elbowed out of the way by a portly Mexican man. From the corner of her eye, Mary saw the guard take a step backward and nod in response to the Mexican's flick of his hand.

Someone important, then.

The Mexican nodded to her. Not quite a bow, but almost. It was something, anyway.

He lifted an arm and gestured to the side. "This way, Señorita," he said.

She knew enough Spanish to correct him. *"Señora,"* she said. "Missus. Mrs. Samuel Teach."

Oddly, the Mexican blinked rapidly, but then recovered. "Señora Teach, then," he said. "This way, if you please?"

Mary didn't question him. She simply went, drawing Becky along with her. The crowd of men parted before them. There were a few laughs and whispers and grumbles and even a catcall or two, but they were all muted.

They made their way into a side room off the big courtyard. It was a library, perhaps, filled with leather chairs, books in ornately carved bookcases, and a massive mahogany desk, carved in the Spanish style. The room bore as much resemblance to their previous lodgings as a palace to the bottom of a dry well.

She settled Becky into a chair, where the girl immediately collapsed into sobs too long held back. Mary heard the door click closed behind them and, still touching Becky's shoulder, turned toward it.

They were not alone. The Mexican was still there, alone, without an accompanying guard. Silently, he crossed the room and sat behind the desk. He regarded her for a long moment, during which the only sounds were those of Becky's keening, and then he gestured at her to come closer.

Señor Carlos Ruiz Lopez templed his fingers as the petite, blue-eyed woman, the wife of former cavalry officer Sam Teach, from whom he had bought his fine Hereford bull, stepped forward. He gestured at her, and she stopped. She looked to be a plucky female, despite the bruises discoloring her cheek and neck. She looked to have been much abused, as did the young girl behind her. Although she was short of stature, she managed to stand straight and tall. At her sides, her hands were balled into delicate but angry fists.

He could not say that he blamed her.

She presented quite a problem, this Mrs. Samuel Teach. One might even say a moral dilemma. He liked her husband. He had shared brandy with him and laughed with him. They had done business together.

And now she was here, standing before him, about to go on the sale block.

It was a very touchy situation, and one he was not prepared to deal with. At least, not at the moment. He steepled his fingers again, and tapped the tips of his forefingers together.

First things first. "You are Mrs. Teach. And this girl is . . . ?"

"B-Becky," stammered the girl. "Rebecca Lowell."

"What you have said is true, Mrs. Teach?" he asked. "Has Miss Lowell lost her mother here, under my roof?"

Mrs. Teach nodded curtly. "It is true. We laid the body out downstairs."

"What happened?"

"As if you c-care!" wailed the girl.

"*¡Silencio!*" he thundered automatically. He was unaccustomed to female outbursts, especially outbursts from servants or chattel.

"Sir!" said Mrs. Teach.

And miraculously, Lopez bit his tongue. He took a deep breath and asked again. "How did this girl's mother die?"

Mary Teach spoke right up. "She was repeatedly beaten and raped by those animals who kidnapped us," the women said angrily. "They pummeled the senses out of her, poor thing. And downstairs, in those group baths of yours, she just . . . She just slipped beneath the water."

By this time, the young girl behind Mrs. Teach was keening again. Lopez ignored her. "I see," he said. "I am very sorry."

"Oh, really?" said Mrs. Teach, her brow arched, her tone sarcastic. He had underestimated her. He had thought her plucky, but now he was thinking it was more than that, much more.

"Are you sorry that they raped her, raped me? Raped us over and over?" Mary Teach went on. Her eyes were dry. Her face was stony in its icy rage, a rage that was just beginning to surface. "Are you sorry that they killed one of us on the trail?"

"Poor Nellie," cried the girl to no one in particular. "Poor Mama."

"I do not know what you are talking about, Señora," he said.

"And it has just occurred to me than you have not introduced yourself," she snapped back.

Lopez pressed his lips together tightly and glared at her. "Forgive me for being discourteous," he said at last, rather flatly. "I'm sure you understand my reluctance to be completely forthcoming."

He stood up rather suddenly, and the woman blinked. Good.

He walked to the door, opened it, and called for Montoya. Mrs. Teach appeared apprehensive, but was making a valiant attempt to cover it.

When Montoya stepped into the room, she looked right at Lopez, lifted her chin, and said, "My husband and I have friends in Mexico, you know. Powerful friends."

He thought he detected a tinge of desperation in her voice. "And that would be . . . ?"

"Señor Carlos Ruiz Lopez," she said. "My husband

recently sold him our bull. Señor Lopez won't be happy to hear what has happened to me."

Beside him, Montoya opened his mouth, but a cutting look from Lopez put an end to that. He said, "I am certain you are correct, Señora Teach." Then, quickly and in Spanish, he ordered Montoya to take the two women upstairs to the third bedroom and lock them in.

To the women, he said, "Go with him. There will be no sale for you tonight."

The girl—what was her name? Becky, that was it, Becky Lowell. She looked up, her face streaked with tears, and she looked relieved. Mrs. Teach simply appeared shocked.

"What are you going to do with us?" Mrs. Teach asked, and her voice was a little higher, her tone a little thinner than before. She thought she knew exactly what he had planned for her, he suspected. And she was probably correct.

But all he said was, "You will go with Señor Montoya. If you have not eaten, you will be brought food and drink."

Mrs. Teach opened her mouth, only uttering a surprised "But—" before Montoya grabbed her arm and the girl's and pulled from the room.

"Gently, Montoya," Lopez said in Spanish as Montoya took them through the doorway. "Gently."

He closed the door behind him, walked back across the room, and slumped behind his desk. What to do now? He could not countenance the sale of Sam Teach's wife. But then, neither could he let her go.

There was a rap at his door, followed by the face of Diego himself. He looked decidedly older than he had all those years ago, but he had aged well. He was tall and lean and gray at the temples, but his mustache was still dark and luxuriant. Constanza and the girls, he thought, had had secret crushes on him for years. Of course, none of them knew his true character, and Lopez was not about to tell them.

"It is time for the sale to begin, Carlos," Diego said rather impatiently. "The buyers, they are getting anxious."

"Tomorrow," Lopez said, "you and I need to have a little talk."

Diego lifted a brow. "About what?"

"It will wait," Lopez replied. "Tomorrow is soon enough." It would also give him time to plan his strategy for breaking the news of his impending retirement. Breaking it so gently, he hoped, that Diego would think he was doing him a favor.

Lopez rose slowly, tugged at his vest, then adjusted his string tie. "Very well, then, Diego. Let us begin."

13

During the night, Sam Teach had been the recipient of a miracle, or so he believed.

He didn't exactly think that God was on his side, although for once, He certainly could have been on Mary's. It would have been awfully nice to have some divine intervention for a change. But considering that the Lord had been looking the other way ever since this bloody bastard of a thing had begun, Sam attributed it to just plain luck.

He'd just slept right, that was all.

Slept so that the slug in his spine had shifted just enough, shifted the right way, so that now he was totally without pain.

He lay there for a few moments in the predawn chill, not believing, certain he was dreaming. At first he moved his fingers, cautiously at first, and then, grinning, flapped his hands like wings.

No pain at all.

He sat up, then stood up, then hopped in a circle. Hopped right on top of Will's hand.

Will came awake in a hurry and had his pistol drawn before he realized it who it was.

"Captain!" he shouted, and scrambled to his feet, blinking.

"You're not dreaming, old friend," Teach said, his hands pounding the big man's shoulders happily. "It was during the night. Something shifted, I guess. I'm not asking any questions."

"Something shifts, it's bound to shift back," said a voice behind him.

Garner. Teach had forgotten all about him and the boy.

But then, who could blame him, seeing as how he was the sole proprietor of a wonderful twist of fate? He turned toward Garner's voice. The old lawman was just standing up, all creaky-like, letting his blankets fall around him.

"Maybe so, Garner," he said, "but like I said, I'm not going to question it." He grinned wide, and his hands balled into fists. "Hell, I'm betting we'll make Galgo today!"

Will muttered, "Not unless we gallop these horses straight into the ground."

Garner didn't say anything. He just stared at Teach for a few seconds, then kicked at his companion, who was sleepily looking up from his bedroll.

"Get crackin', Hobie," was all he said.

While Hobie busied himself with the making of breakfast, Garner saw to their horses. This thing about Teach— the man just standing right up like everything was peachy keen—was beyond him.

Why, yesterday, the man had looked like he wouldn't make it until this morning, let alone past midnight! Right now, as the sun was sending tentative fingers of soft orange and pale pink up into a violet sky, Teach was gathering up bedrolls, bending and squatting and rolling up blankets like nothing was wrong.

"Damnedest thing I've ever seen," muttered Will, who was brushing down Shorty, two horses over from Garner. He looked up. "I mean, have you ever seen the likes of it?"

Garner shook his head in the negative. "I meant what I said, though." He made a last pass over Faro with the body brush, then picked up the curry comb and started on Fly. "About it turnin' around on him. Probably when he's least expecting it."

"But it's gone for now," Will said mulishly. "He hasn't looked so spry in weeks. Ain't asked for the laudanum once this morning, neither."

"Uh-huh," said Garner.

Will stopped brushing and rested his arms on the horse's back. "What are you tryin' to say, Garner?"

"Already said it," Garner replied. "Nothing more to it."

Will grunted and went back to work.

Garner finished brushing down Fly, and at about the exact moment he put down the last of his hooves, freshly picked, Hobie hollered that breakfast was ready. Garner lingered by the horses, though. He didn't quite know what to make of this new situation. Frankly, he'd figured that he and Hobie would just ride on out on their own this morning. They'd have a better chance of finding those women, if they were still alive.

And they'd have a better chance of effecting the women's freedom, too, if the truth were to be told. Besides being stove up, Sam Teach was too deeply invested in this thing. His wife was one of the captives, after all. He had no business being out here in the first place, even if he hadn't been hurt.

Which, of course, Teach wasn't, now, was he?

Sort of threw a hoe handle through the old wagon-wheel spokes.

•　•　•

At roughly an hour after dawn, Mary heard a key turn in the locked door of their room and snapped to attention. Becky was asleep on the enormous, carved bed, and Mary gave her a quicky thump.

"What?" Becky said groggily just as the door opened.

There was a guard, who remained beside the door, a rifle in his hands. But there was also a pretty little Mexican serving girl, who bore a covered tray.

This, she silently rested upon a table in a corner of the large room, and whisked away the covering napkin. Mary's mouth, despite everything, immediately began to water.

The girl, who apparently spoke no English, said something totally unintelligible to Mary, smiled, curtsied, and took her leave. The guard, whose attitude and countenance were not nearly so pleasant as the girl's, locked the door behind her, leaving Mary and Becky alone.

"Gee!" Becky said with a yawn. She sat up and scooted off the high bed. "Look at that!"

There were scrambled eggs with onions and bits of red peppers, bacon, sausages, and warm tortillas, along with corn muffins and strawberry jam—and, oddly enough, a large bowl of refried beans covered in what looked like melted goat cheese—all served on the finest silver.

A carafe of water and another of milk had been provided to wash it down.

Becky hurried to the table and had gobbled a muffin before she remembered herself and stopped. Mouth full of crumbs, she sheepishly asked, "Is it all right to eat? They're not going to poison us, are they?"

Mary shrugged. Last night, she had made Becky refuse the dinner that had been brought to them, for fear it would be drugged. It would be an easy thing, she had thought, for their host, after promising them limited sanctuary, to drug them, then pack them off to parts unknown. Like Chile or Argentina.

Or Jesus.

But Becky had already swallowed half the muffin. It didn't matter now, Mary supposed. Besides, the auction was long over.

"Go ahead," Mary said. "Eat."

She joined Becky at the table, although she took a seat and unfolded one of the provided napkins before she reached for a muffin. This, she washed down with a big glass of fresh milk.

Without thinking, she softly patted her stomach. "That's for you, little one," she whispered.

"What?" asked Becky. Her mouth was full of beans this time. She had piled bacon, eggs, and a huge scoop of refried beans atop a tortilla, folded it in half, and was attempting to eat it without getting it all over herself, the table, and the floor.

"Nothing," Mary said, and then snapped, "Didn't your mother teach you any manners?"

She immediately felt awful, because at the mention of the word *mother*, Becky's eyes filled with tears.

Mary reached across the table and grasped the girl's wrist. "I'm so sorry, honey. But there's been so much . . . so much to worry about. Still is. I'm sorry I snapped."

"S'okay," Becky sniffed, and after a moment, she scrubbed at her eyes, then went back to work on her breakfast.

The young are so resilient, thought Mary with a shake of her head. This girl had been through every horror imaginable. And still she was merrily eating as if today, someone was going to present her with a white charger, a picnic lunch, a map and a compass, and just let her ride away.

Mary, on the other hand, found herself thinking more and more like . . . well, like a man. Like Sam would think, she hoped. If he couldn't be here for her, she would have to try to *be* him. As they ate, she stared out the window, making note of the surrounding terrain, the number of men—those that she could see, at any rate—and the outbuildings, their locations, and what she assumed they were used for. She tried to think of every possibility. There, in the smallish shed—tool storage, perhaps? Could they hide there? If they managed to climb out this window, that is. They were on the second floor, and had a straight drop down.

But assuming they could escape the house, where would they go from there? They would need horses. They would need food. They would also need some kind of weapons.

Mary'd had no need to shoot a gun in years, but she thought she still could. Her father had taught her when she was a girl and they lived on the wild prairies of Kansas. When she was nine, she had shot an attacking Pawnee off his pony, killing him instantly at forty paces.

It had been a long, long time ago, but she had no compunctions about aiming at—and shooting—people, especially when those people were about to kill her or those she loved.

She continued to stare out the window, chewing and thinking.

Thinking what Sam would do.

Lopez, seated at his desk and shifting through a thick ledger, finally found what he was looking for. He rose, left the office, and went in search of Montoya. He found him in the kitchen, his boots up on the table, holding a giggling, squealing chambermaid in his lap.

Lopez cleared his throat.

The girl flushed and immediately jumped free, and Montoya's boots hit the floor. He stood quickly. *"¿Patrón?"* he said. At least he had the good sense to look a little embarrassed.

"Go into town," Lopez said without further preamble.

"Find me the men who consigned the two women upstairs. Two Americans named Smeed and Chambers."

Montoya looked confused. "But tomorrow is the day
we pay, Señor. It has always been the second day after the
auction. You must do the bookkeeping."

"Find them," Lopez repeated. "I intend to pay them
today. But perhaps not in the coin they expect."

With that, Lopez turned on his heel and went back out
into the hacienda, back to his office. He was, if nothing
else, a man of honor. At least, he was trying to change
himself back into one. This had been the first step, sending Montoya out like a well-trained dog.

The next would be his confrontation with Diego, who
was still asleep upstairs, probably with two, perhaps three
naked women in his bed.

He would let him linger until noon, and then they
would talk.

He hoped it could be kept to talk, anyway.

14

When they stopped around midday for lunch and to rest the horses, Garner still hadn't figured out how to politely get shed of Sam Teach and Will Thurlow. He was beginning to think the best thing to do would just be to ride off and leave them flat: no excuses offered, just go.

Except there was Hobie to consider, dammit. Hobie'd have a fit and he'd never hear the end of it. Plus which, Will and Teach seemed to know the way to Galgo just as well as he did.

No, it wouldn't do him any damn good at all to ditch them. He'd be roasted on a spit if he knew what to do, but he had a feeling that Sam Teach, in his ardor, was going to get them all killed.

For not the first time—nor for the last, very probably—he mentally kicked himself in the backside for ever answering Hobie's telegram.

"What?" asked Hobie, startling him.

Garner frowned.

Hobie nodded toward Garner's hand. He had forgotten he was holding his plate, and beans were slowly dripping

from the tilted rim of it. He set it down on the ground beside him.

"Nothing," he said.

"Oh, sure," said Hobie. "I always pour my dinner in
the dirt for nothin'."

Garner ignored him. Instead, he stared over toward the
horses, where both Teach and Will were fussing with
their mounts. They had already finished their meals, as
had Hobie. Garner had been less than pleasant company,
having been lost in his thoughts.

Suddenly, he twisted back toward Hobie. "If you've
got half a brain," he said quietly, "you'll go home. Right
now."

Hobie's face twisted. "Huh? What the heck are you
talkin' about, Boss?"

"This is a regular idiot's errand, boy," Garner said. "If
that wife of Teach's isn't dead already, she's on her way
to Brazil or Peru or someplace. And us going down to
Galgo, trying to find her, is going to be the end of all of
us."

Hobie's features relaxed from puzzlement, and then
into disbelief. "Now, Boss, how the heck you figure that?
There's four of us now, and it ain't like that time we went
after Donny Belasco. This time, the men we got are all
good! No newspaper scribblers, no show-off lawmen.
Two former members of the danged United States Cavalry is what we've got! Now, I don't know what that
means to you, but what it says to me is that they're both
pretty handy with firearms, and can hold their own in a
fight."

Garner shook his head. "You've never been to Galgo,
have you, Hobie?"

"Course not. You know I never been to Mexico."

"It's a tough town. As tough as they come. This auction has been going on for years, except nobody seems to
know just where it's held, or, leastwise, admits to know-

ing. Good men—well-meaning types—have tried, and ended up murdered for their trouble."

"But Boss . . ." Hobie broke in.

Garner held up a hand. "Sam Teach is too close to the thing to see straight, and from what I can figure, the only reason Will Thurlow's along is out of loyalty to Teach. Will thinks she's dead, too. Or worse. Teach is going to do something stupid, sooner if not later, that's going to send us all home to Jesus. Or down to someplace else. Rather not see that happen to you."

Hobie suddenly stood up and grabbed Garner's plate and coffee cup. "Fine," he said. "I'll just go home with my tail tucked betwixt my legs, then." He angrily scraped Garner's plate into the brittle weeds, and tossed the cold coffee after it. A sparrow immediately landed and began to feast. "But while I'm mindin' you and desertin' this mess, what are you gonna be doing?"

When there was no reply, Hobie shook his head. "It figures. It just figures. You're gonna go right on ahead and ride down there with these fellers, ain't you? I ain't as dumb as you think I am, Boss. And I can make up my mind all by myself. Once we ride off that ranch of yours, I ain't working for you, I'm workin' with you. Equals. In fact, if you remember, I got my badge handed to me first, so maybe that makes me your superior."

Slowly, Garner rose to his feet. "Hobie, unless you want to get your teeth all full of my fist, you'd better—"

"What's going on over here?" asked Sam Teach, halfway back from the horses and followed directly by Will Thurlow.

Garner glared at Hobie and ground his teeth. "Nothing," he said tersely. "Nothing except we're wasting daylight."

"My thoughts exactly," said Teach. "We're close. The horses are holding up well. We can be in Galgo sometime after dark, if the moon doesn't cloud over."

"Right you are, Captain," said Will, although without much enthusiasm.

"Right," said Hobie, and slid a cutting glance in Garner's direction.

"Shit," Garner grumbled, and stalked off toward the horses.

"You sure you're still all right, Captain?" Will asked. He had to shout, as he was trailing a little behind the Captain, and traveling at a slow lope. One thing about this King Garner, he knew how to pace a horse, get the most out of it with the least harm. Will admired him for it. In his time, he'd seen many an overeager lieutenant gallop his troops straight into the ground.

"Fine!" the Captain shouted back. "Just dandy!"

Indeed, he seemed to be in a fine fettle. Whatever had shifted that fraction of an inch in his backbone had seemed to lift his spirits—and raise his hopes—higher than the church steeple back in town.

Will was certain-sure they were going to be crushed, and that made him sadder than anything, almost as sad as if he'd lost one of his own kids, or his Bess.

Ahead, Garner raised a hand, signaling them to slow down to a jog once more. Will knew Garner's pattern pretty well by this time. It was the one he would have followed himself. Walk for a while, jog for a while, lope for a mile or two, then back down to a jog, then a walk, then stop to water the horses and give them a breather.

Their horses never built up a real lather, never got winded, and they just kept on going. Forever, it seemed to Will.

And the Captain had been right. They would reach Galgo tonight. Around seven or eight, if Will was any judge. There were no clouds in the sky, and he'd bet anything that the moon would be round and high and bright enough to guide them safely over just about any land-scape.

Damn it, anyway.

By four o'clock that afternoon, Diego was still upstairs with his girls, blast his randy hide, but Montoya had just returned.

He had with him not both of the men in question, but only one, who appeared to have been involved in a fight. Not with Montoya, because the bruises weren't that fresh. Any Montoya had put on him would show up later, and Lopez was certain that by tomorrow, he would be quite a colorful character.

Literally.

Lopez sat behind his desk, and Montoya thrust the hapless man into an armchair opposite, then retired to stand in front of the door, arms crossed.

"And which one are you?" Lopez asked.

"Screw you," grumbled the man through swollen lips. "I don't know why he had to beat me up. I would'a come. You owe me money, don't you?"

Lopez raised his eyes. "Montoya?"

The man in the chair cringed.

"Smeed," Montoya said. "Ike Smeed. The one called Chambers was nowhere to be found. But he will come of his own accord tomorrow." He smiled. "I can almost promise it. I have spread word that his women sold for a great deal of money, by private treaty."

Diego nodded. "Excellent, Montoya! That will explain why they did not appear on the block."

Montoya tipped his head. *"Gracias, señor."*

Smeed's dark features twisted angrily. "Hey, what's goin' on here? What the hell are you people tryin' to pull?"

Smeed started to rise and Montoya took a step toward him, but Lopez waved them both down. It was odd,

Lopez thought. He was the smallest man in the room, yet rank and social standing seemed to impress and cow even a man like Smeed, for he sat back down.

Now, Lopez had been doing quite a bit of thinking while he waited for Montoya to come back—or conversely, for that fool Diego to come downstairs. He had almost come to the conclusion that he must return the women. He would contact Sam Teach and tell him to come get his wife. He would apologize. He would grovel, if necessary.

He was well aware that the United States authorities could do nothing to him. The Mexican authorities were something else entirely, but he was fairly certain a few well-placed—and very large—bribes would cool things down.

Diego, though? That was another matter. He only wished that the pig had come downstairs from his debauchery. He had gone up to get him once, and heard the giggles and groaning mattress from the other side of the door. He hadn't knocked. He did not wish to be reminded of the end result of the business he had gotten himself into.

Or rather, that Diego had coerced him into undertaking.

"Señor Smeed," he said at last, "it is my understanding that you brought us the females called Mary Teach and Becky Lowell."

"I guess," Smeed said sullenly. His left eye, the one that was not already purple, was beginning to pinken and swell. Montoya's handiwork just beginning to bloom, no doubt. "And the other one. The old bat."

"Ah, yes," Lopez said. Suddenly, he wished to ask Montoya to leave the room and have a little fun with Smeed himself. The man disgusted him.

Almost, in fact, as much as he disgusted himself.

"The mother of the girl," said Lopez. "A Mrs. Agatha Lowell."

Smeed shrugged, then winced. There must be many bruises beneath his clothing, too. "What about it?" Smeed asked. "When do we get our money?"

Lopez clicked his tongue. "I am sorry to tell you, Señor Smeed, but there will be no payment."

"What?" Smeed bellowed, forgetting himself. Immediately Montoya was behind him, pushing him back down into the chair. He sat, but he didn't stop being irate. "Why the hell not?" he spat.

Lopez kept his voice soft and even. "Because, Señor Smeed, Mrs. Lowell did not survive to see the auction. It seems that you and your partner, Señor Chambers, brutalized all of these women. Brutalized Mrs. Lowell to the point where she lost her mind. She drowned herself here, in the bath."

"But she was delivered, goddamn it!" Smeed cried. If Lopez was any judge, the man was beginning to look a little worried. "What about them other two? They was still in decent shape, wasn't they? Look, we went to a lot of trouble to—"

"Oh," Lopez broke in, "I could tell that you had a great deal of trouble with them. This was why you felt the need to repeatedly rape Mrs. Teach and beat them both, no?"

Smeed shrank back just a little in his chair. His bravado was fading quickly now. He didn't answer.

"It is also my understanding that there was a fourth women, a women you murdered on the trail."

Again, Smeed was silent. Mary Teach had told the truth, then, about everything.

Lopez sat back in his chair and went about the business of lighting one of his excellent Cuban cigars. As he clipped the end off, he said, "Your friend, Chambers. Where might we locate him?"

Smeed remained silent, and at a nod from Lopez, who was striking a match, Montoya put his hand on Smeed's shoulder and began to squeeze.

Hard.

Smeed was tough, though. Tears welled in his eyes before he finally blurted out, "He's out ridin' around, all right? I don't know where. We got into a fight in a bar last night, and the damn coward just doffed his hat and stepped out, left me to take on four fellers all by my lonesome. When I went down to the stable later, his horse was gone. That's all I know, goddamn it!" he cried. "Tell this overgrown monkey to quit! I heard something pop in my shoulder!"

Lopez nodded, and Montoya backed off.

Lopez shook out his match.

He held out his cigar box to Smeed.

"A last cigar, Señor?"

Smeed had eagerly taken one before he paused, fingers trembling. "Did you say a last one?" he asked, voice quavering.

"Yes, I did," Lopez said quietly. "Montoya, would you please clip that cigar and light it for Señor Smeed? He looks a bit shaky to me."

Smeed just stared at him.

"You see, my dear Smeed, once you have finished your cigar, Montoya will take you out back to the butchering shed and shoot you."

When Smeed visibly paled, Lopez added, "Oh, it will be all right. Do not fear that you will go to waste. Your meat will be ground into meat meal, your bones ground into bone meal, and all will be fed to the chickens. Nothing goes to waste here on my rancho. We give the same treatment to the carcasses of any vermin we happen to kill."

Grinning, Montoya jabbed the Havana between Smeed's swollen, trembling lips and lit it.

15

Chambers sat on a high rock, his rifle slung casually across his knees, his horse tethered to a scrubby tree far below, behind him. He never went anywhere without the rifle. It was his pet.

This would be the last time, he told himself. Never again would he partner with Ike Smeed, the pig.

It wasn't that he had anything against Smeed for his treatment of women. No, that was fine by him. Actually, he enjoyed it, to a degree. But the fact still irked him that, for practically no discernible purpose other than that stupid little knife she'd had, Smeed had killed their best sales prospect, the whore called Nellie.

And it also pissed him off that Smeed somehow managed to pick a fight with every damn person they ran across. Take that fight last night, for example.

Stupid, just plain stupid. And this time, he hadn't stuck around to help Smeed get his tit out of the wringer. No, he'd just slipped out the back and sauntered down to the livery, picked up his horse, and ridden out of town, free as a lark and with no fresh bruises. A night under the stars sure as hell beat waking up all busted up.

Again.

On the other hand, maybe Ike was in jail. Now there was a happy thought! Maybe he was in a cell, and Chambers could go pick up the cash tomorrow and just skip town.

On second thought, though, he didn't think that Galgo had anything like a lawman, let alone a jail. Even he, who was accustomed to raw, rough towns, had been a little taken aback when they first rode into town.

Not that he'd let Smeed know, of course.

Hell, Smeed had never seemed so goddamned happy to see anyplace, at least not since Chambers had been riding with him. And Smeed was even happier when he was picking a fight, insulting some stranger on purpose and really grinding it in, for no other reason than to start a brawl.

The first night in town, Chambers had figured out pretty damned quick that Galgo wasn't a place where you wanted to get into a fracas, but Smeed, the stupid sonofabitch, had had a high old time. And they both had the bruises to prove it.

Well, enough of that.

Tomorrow, Montoya, the man they'd turned their women over to, would pay them. He'd pay everybody, that was the usual deal. He'd set up at a table at the Tres Lobos Cantina, get out his list and his cash box, and the consignors would line up, hats in hands, to have their money counted out. Chambers had done this before. He knew the routine.

And Chambers couldn't wait to find out just how much those three hens had brought. He figured they'd get the most for that little Becky gal. She was the least beat up, anyhow, and it had been some kind of hard work to keep her a virgin. Of course, all she did was cry and whine, but he figured that wasn't his problem.

Then there was Mary. She was sure the prettiest, and also the most compliant. Oh, not so much about the sex. She was so wooden and stiff when he took her that he'd given up on her after a while. It was no fun when they didn't scream or cry. But by God, she knew how to take orders. She did what she was told, and did it without being told more than once. And he'd heard they were big on that, these auction people.

And he figured the least for Mama.

Actually, he'd be surprised if they didn't just hand her back over to him and Smeed and tell them they couldn't sell the cow. Naturally, he blamed this on Smeed, too.

He was watching a circling hawk as he thought this over, watching it drift and wheel on the wind currents high above him, and he wondered if it might be best to get on back to Galgo. It was getting late. There'd be Smeed to contend with, but hell, if that fight-happy idiot started anything with him, Chambers would settle his hash.

Maybe permanently. A happy thought.

The sun had edged toward the horizon while he mulled over just how he might do away with Smeed. More money for *him*, after all. And the circling hawk had long since swooped down to the desert floor, rising again with a fat pack rat wriggling its last in the bird's sharp talons.

Chambers had laughed as it flew away and out of sight.

But he had lingered so long that now it would be dark before he got back to town. There'd be a full moon tonight, though, and the skies were clear. There was time for a little fun.

He brought up the rifle, always as spotless as he himself was filthy. It was equipped with a polished brass telescopic sight, also shined and buffed within an inch of its life. He nestled it against his shoulder. Maybe, if he was lucky, he could kill something before he started back.

Slowly, he scanned the desert floor below, searching for prey. He had just about settled on a lone coyote, and was slowly tightening his finger on the trigger, when the coyote suddenly spooked and sprinted away.

"Bastard," Chambers muttered.

And then he saw what had startled the coyote.

Four men, riding at a slow lope but with a definite purpose, came into range.

Why? he wondered. Nobody in his right mind went to Galgo unless he was going there to do business. This particular direction led to nowhere but Galgo—or the Pacific Ocean—and this year's sale was over and done with.

The only other reason he could think of to go to Galgo was if a man lived there, or if he were a sailor. But none of these men were Mexicans, and they sure as hell didn't ride like any seamen he'd ever seen.

He could make out their faces now. A blond kid on a buckskin; a big, tough-looking hombre riding a bay; and behind them a massive blond man—who he automatically assumed to be a Swede, for some reason—and . . .

Sonofabitch.

He squinted into the scope, pressing his eye close enough to dent his skin in the shape of a ring.

Damn it! It was the same one, all right. He thought he'd killed that peckerwood weeks ago, when they took the first gal! Hell, he'd shot him, and Smeed had shot him, too! No excuse for it, no excuse at all.

This bastard just didn't want to die, that was all. And this filled Chambers with an odd sort of shame. And fury. He had his pride, by God.

Well, the third shot was the charm, wasn't it?

He followed that hard-to-kill bastard with the scope, resting the rifle's long barrel on his cocked knee, and waited for a clear shot. It was going to be tricky, because the Swede was riding in between them. But Chambers knew he could do it.

Hell, shot twice and *still* not dead. Goddamn! He must be the luckiest bastard on the face of the earth.

Chambers followed along until they were less than four hundred yards away. He had a clear shot now.

Smiling, he took it.

Except that in the time it took him to squeeze the trigger, all four horses abruptly slowed down to a jog, and the Swede pulled in between Chambers and his target.

And fell off his horse, clutching at his shoulder.

In a fraction of a second, the other three had stopped and taken cover, but by the time the sound of Chambers's shot could reach them, Chambers had scrambled down the backside of that rock and was slithering down toward his horse. By the time he heard shots being returned, he was already galloping toward Galgo, hidden behind the high rocks.

Of all the rotten, stinking luck!

"Stop firing!" snarled Garner. "Hold up!"

The last echo of their final shot died, and still, no one was returning their fire. Whoever had been up there was gone, all right. Not that it was quiet. If he listened hard, he could just make out the thin echo of distant hoofbeats, galloping, galloping off to the south, growing farther away and fainter all the time.

He got up off his belly, dusted his britches, and tried to shake the kink out of his leg. He'd landed wrong. "How is he?" he called to Teach.

"He'll live," Teach hissed. "And get down, man!"

Hobie was getting up, too, although he was still eyeing the hilltop from which the shot had come.

"No reason," said Garner. He pounded on the side of his knee with his fist, heard something snap, and then it was all right again. "The sonofabitch is long gone. And yes," he added, when Teach opened his mouth to argue, "I'm sure. Heard him riding away. You would have, too, if you'd been listening for it instead of poppin' off rounds like they were pine needles and you owned the forest."

Teach had the good sense to look a little bit pained, and didn't answer.

Garner would have ridden him harder—after all, he'd been a cavalry officer and ought to know better—but he didn't push the subject. Teach had been through hell these last few weeks, and now, to top everything off, his best friend was stove up.

Now, Garner felt two ways about this. He was sorry about Will, who was just sitting up with a little help from Teach. He liked Will. But the thought had crossed his mind that maybe Will wouldn't be in such good shape to ride, and maybe Teach could be talked into staying back and keeping pace with Will, allowing Hobie and Garner to ride on into Galgo well ahead of them.

He really didn't want Teach along for this part, the part that was coming.

"Who the heck you think that was?" Hobie asked.

"Who?"

Hobie made a face. "The feller who just took a shot at us."

Garner had almost forgotten.

"Don't know," he said. "But I'll find out. Sooner or later, I'll find out. Can you round up the horses by yourself?"

They hadn't wandered far, and after taking a quick look around, Hobie said, "Sure, Boss. You'd best check on Will. He don't look too good to me."

Garner would have said something snide about kids giving orders to their elders, but one look at Will told him that the boy was right. He nodded and walked on over.

Teach had ripped away Will's sleeve by that time. Will was white as milk. The slug had taken him high in the shoulder, but it hadn't passed all the way through.

A worried Teach looked over as Garner knelt down. "It's lodged in the joint, I think," said Teach.

"Sure as hell lodged somewhere," Will mumbled through gritted teeth. "Hurts like a blasted branding iron's in there."

Garner reached toward his pocket, at the same time asking, "Got any whiskey on you? For the blade." He pulled out a slim pocketknife. Hobie always told him he kept it sharp enough to slice the brand clean off a steer before it knew what hit it.

"No," Teach said. "None."

"Hobie!" Garner shouted with a turn of his head. "Bring me that little flask of bourbon out of my saddlebags."

Then he turned back toward Will and Teach. "You got any of that poppy juice left?"

Will managed to nod. "Saddlebag," he said.

Garner twisted his head again. "And Will's got some laudanum in his saddlebag. Bring that, too."

Hobie, in the distance, waved that he'd heard. He'd already caught three horses, and looked to be talking his way up to the fourth, who was still a little skittish. It was Will's gelding, Butter Pie.

"Why?" Teach was asking. "Why would somebody shoot at us? Nobody knows we're coming, or why. Nobody even knows who we are! Why would anybody take a shot at Will?"

Garner didn't answer, but Teach's rhetorical questions had gotten him to thinking. Nobody knew who they were, all right, except those fellows who'd kidnapped Teach's wife in the first place, the ones who'd later shot him when he was on his way home. And they'd gotten a good look at his face, from what he'd learned between Will and Teach.

Whoever had shot at them had done it from a good four hundred yards away. He had to be a crack shot, and he had to either have a telescopic sight on that rifle, or else the best pair of eyes that God ever gave man or eagle.

Garner had a fair idea that he'd been aiming for Teach, not Will. As he remembered, Will had been riding on Teach's off side, which would have put him between Teach and the sniper.

If Garner hadn't signaled for a jog just when he had, the rifleman would have most likely hit his target.

And Teach had said it was the one called Chambers who had shot him from a distance before. It must have really pissed the sonofabitch off that Teach wasn't dead.

Garner couldn't figure out what Chambers was doing out here, unless he was on his way back up to Arizona. But his hoofbeats had retreated in the opposite direction, toward Galgo.

They had enough problems for the time being, and he didn't need Teach any madder or more upset than he already was, and so he didn't say anything. But he sure had a pretty damned good idea who the shooter had been.

Hobie led the horses up, and handed over a canteen, with which Teach washed Will's arm, and then the laudanum.

When Hobie handed down the flask, Garner took it, but didn't open it. He'd wait for the laudanum to kick in before he started digging around in there. He just hoped the slug was situated where it would pop out easy.

He imagined that Will was hoping the same thing, and with a lot more fervor than *he* was.

"Don't be a piker, Teach," he said. "Give him another drink of it."

Teach did.

And hadn't it been a goddamn miracle that Teach had jumped clean off his horse and hit the ground rolling without that slug in his back inching over any at all?

Shit.

16

It was nearing dark by the time Diego deigned to make an
appearance. He was just coming down the stairs, dressed
haphazardly and shouting for food, when he ran into
Lopez.

Or rather, Lopez ran into him.

"We need to talk, old friend," Lopez said, forcing a
friendly smile.

"Ah, you must have the receipts in order," Diego said
with a grin. "But food first, then we talk. Ah, such a day
I have had, Lopez!" he added, leering and casting his
eyes upward, toward his room. "I cannot tell you!"

"I assure you, there is no need," Lopez replied. He
looped his arm over the taller man's shoulders. "Let me
order us both an early supper, and while it is being prepared, we will talk."

Diego tipped his head and shrugged. "Whatever you
say, *compadre*. But it had better be a good dinner."

Lopez nodded at the cook, who had come from the
kitchen at Diego's shout, and she nodded in reply.

"There, you see?" Lopez said, still all warm smiles and friendship. "Let us have a brandy and talk business."

"After you," said Diego.

Lopez in the lead, they started for the study.

Garner got his wish.

After a sufficient dose of laudanum, Will had passed out. It was a lot less trouble digging a stubborn slug out of an unconscious man's shoulder than that of the poor bastard who screamed and thrashed through the whole thing.

The entire process took Garner less than five minutes. He flipped the slug into the dirt, poured the rest of the bourbon into the wound and over Will's shoulder, and bandaged him with one of Hobie's extra shirts, ripped into strips.

He got to his feet and thumbed back his hat. "That'll hold him till he gets to a real doc," he said. He looked up at the sky, at the setting sun. "He can't travel," he said to Teach. "Not till morning, at least."

Teach frowned. "We'll have to wait, then."

"No, *you'll* have to wait. Me and Hobie are riding on ahead."

"We are, Boss?" Hobie piped up. Garner knew the kid well enough to figure that they'd both been thinking along the same lines. One glance at the boy told him he was right. Hobie's expression told him that he'd be all the happier to leave Teach—their liability—temporarily behind.

"No!" shouted Teach, and leapt to his feet so quickly that even Garner was surprised. Hobie's eyes bugged out a little.

"You will not . . ." Teach began. And then a pained expression came over his face. He bent slightly. "You can't leave me here when Mary is so close," he said, gasping, as he sank to his knees. One hand went to his back while the other braced him, kept him from falling over on his side.

"Damn," Garner heard him whisper. "Why, God, why now?"

Garner knelt down to him. "You okay, Teach?"

Through gritted teeth, Teach said, "Of course I'm not, you idiot! The damned slug moved again!"

"I know that, you stubborn jackass," replied Garner. "I mean, will you be all right out here alone with Will? We'll leave you water and grub. And we'll bring a wagon back for you."

"Goddamn you, Garner," Teach hissed.

"I'll take that for a yes," Garner replied, and stood up. "Hobie?"

"Right here, Boss." The kid was already standing there, holding out two canteens, a canvas water bag, and one of their food sacks. He put everything on the ground, within Teach's reach. "I'll get a fire goin' for you before we leave, Captain Teach," he said. "Sorry about your back." And with the touch of a finger to the brim of his hat, he went off to gather firewood.

Garner just shook his head.

"Well, you got your way, didn't you, you son-ofabitch?" Teach asked. His voice sounded thin, strangled.

"Where's that laudanum?" Garner asked, ignoring the question. He scooped up the bottle from the dirt beside Will, who was still out cold, and uncorked it. He held it out to Teach. "One swallow," he said. "It's almost gone. Guess I kind of overdosed Will."

Teach obeyed, but not happily.

"We'll try to find more in Galgo," Garner said. "But make that last as long as you can. And lie down, for Christ's sake. You're makin' me hurt, seeing you all propped up crooked like that."

Teach eased himself all the way down to the ground. "I'd like to make you hurt, all right."

"I'll bet you would."

Hobie showed up with kindling and enough firewood to last them the night, and while he started a fire and set the coffee to brewing, Garner stripped the tack off Will and Teach's horses, hobbled, watered, and fed them. Fly and Faro didn't take too kindly to being left out, but they might be in for a little hard riding before the day was over. There'd be time enough to rest when they got to Galgo.

He tightened their girths, Hobie having loosened them once he'd seen they were going to be stopped here for a while, and led them toward the fire. The sky was beginning to color up in the west. There wouldn't be light for much longer.

"Ready?" he asked Hobie.

The kid stood up. "Just let me get the Captain's bedroll from his pack, and I'll be right with you."

While Hobie ran to fetch the blankets as well as the saddles to serve as Teach and Will's pillows, Teach looked up at Garner. The laudanum was starting to take effect, and some of the lines of pain were easing from his face.

"Find her, Garner," he said, his voice still ragged around the edges. "Go to my friend, Carlos Ruiz Lopez."

"I know. You told me. You sold him a bull."

"He might know about these auctions. Or these men." He took a halting breath, then repeated, "Find her."

Garner couldn't tell if it was a plea or a command. He doubted if Teach knew, either. But he tried to smile, and said, "I didn't ride all the way down here for the enchiladas, Teach."

Teach closed his eyes for a moment. "I'm sorry," he said. "It's just . . ."

"I know," Garner replied. "If she's to be found, we'll bring her back."

Teach just nodded, then turned his head away.

Garner mounted Faro. "Hurry up, Hobie!" he hollered, just for an excuse to look away from Teach.

"Comin', Boss!" Hobie called. "I'm comin' as fast as I can!"

Montoya had at last finished his labors. The late Ike Smeed had died like a woman, down on his knees and begging for his life. Which had absolutely no effect on Montoya. He did what he was told, and he liked his work. Perhaps he liked it a little too much.

Smeed was now no more than ground-up bone and ground-up meat, and the innards had gone to feed the hogs. Montoya had smoked while he watched them tussling over the intestines, yanking on them like men in a tug-of-war.

The liver, brains, and kidneys had gone first, Montoya had noted. Even hogs could be connoisseurs at times, he supposed.

When they had finished arguing over the innards, he took pity on them and brought out a bucket full of ground meat, too. There was too much to spread out and dry, anyway—after all, there was more to a man than a skinny coyote.

Smeed's clothing and personal effects had been burned in the big furnace over at the smithy, and his one valuable possession, a molar made of gold, now resided in Montoya's pocket.

Montoya washed up at the pump beside the corral's water trough, then went over and sat on a stump beside the butchering shed to watch the sun set.

There was a great deal of satisfaction to be had in a job well done, he thought as he lazily rolled a cigarette, then stuck it between his lips. He struck a match.

Yes, he thought, a great deal of satisfaction. He listened to the everyday sounds of the cattle down in the big barn lowing, heard the saddle horses whinnying for their supper. Quite faintly, he could hear the sea crashing against the cliffs. He inhaled the cigarette smoke deep into his lungs, and smiled.

The sunset was very nice tonight.

"No," said Diego, just that flatly.

After all the time Lopez had taken to explain the situation, he had expected a longer speech, or at least a few moments of thought.

"Did you hear anything that I said?" Lopez asked angrily. "I have paid my debt to you. Find another house to hold your auctions. I want no more to do with it, or its dirty profit."

"Ah, Carlos," Diego said with a slow shake of his handsome head. "You disappoint me. Just when I was beginning to think you were truly enjoying our little arrangement."

"I have never enjoyed it in all these years."

Diego took a long, slow look around the study, at the rich furnishings, the fine paintings, the expensive fabric draping the windows. He looked back at Lopez. "It would seem you have enjoyed the profits from it, *amigo*."

Lopez winced a little at that *amigo*. This man had never, never been his friend. But he wisely withheld comment and said, "I want to get out, Diego. Surely, you can see that I—"

"All I see is a house perfect for our little business," Diego replied, helping himself to a cigar from the humidor. "I see a town with no law, an old Spanish prison perfect for holding our inventory until the sales, and besides, everyone who matters—to us and our business, anyway—knows exactly where to come for the type of goods they are searching for.

"Besides," he added as he clipped the end off his cigar, "while you have been building your hacienda with your money, sending your family away on extended trips, and buying fancy cattle, I have—foolishly, I admit, but with the utmost enjoyment—frittered mine away on the pleasures of life. And by the way, I no longer have a hacienda of my own. I fear that a bad turn of cards has taken that. No, the sale stays here. Nothing changes." He paused to light his cigar, and then his tone changed. "You know what will happen if you press this."

"Do not threaten me, Diego," Lopez said, his voice just as serious as Diego's, although, beneath the desk, he was gripping the arms of his chair so tightly that he feared they would splinter in his grasp. "That was a very long time ago. Now I have friends in high places. A great more than do you, I should say. And there is something I have not told you."

Diego studied the ember on the end of his cigar, blasé as ever, damn him. "And what, dear Lopez, might that be?"

"I have, upstairs, two women which I have withheld from the sale. Our consignors no longer buy young girls from poor families and bring them, untouched, to me. These past years, it has been growing worse and worse. It is now degraded to the point that they kidnap women, brutalize them, and then bring them here, expecting me to sell them."

Diego shrugged. "And what is this to me?"

"It should mean a great deal to you, Diego. One of the women currently lodging in my guest quarters is the wife of an American, a former cavalry officer with whom I have done business."

Diego clucked his tongue, but said nothing. His expression told Lopez that Diego didn't give a damn. It was like trying to convince a wall to move over a foot or two, just for a minute. But still, Lopez didn't give up.

"The books are finished, and the money counting is done," he continued. He made himself let go of one arm of the chair, and from a drawer, brought up a fat bag of coins that he plopped on the desk.

"Your share," he said, and when Diego's eyebrows lifted at the size of the plunder, Lopez added, "and mine as well. Take it all. I will have no more part in this."

Diego stood up. He lifted the heavy bag and hefted it admiringly. "This is very kind of you, Lopez, very kind indeed. And I shall take you up on it. The money, that is. But the sales will go on. And you will dispose of those women upstairs."

Lopez stood up, his hands balled into fists. "No. I will not. This is my final word."

"I do not believe so, *amigo,*" Diego said, and swiftly brought the bag of coins up.

The last sensation Lopez remembered was not the pain, not the jarring concussion as the bag hit the side of his head, but the sound.

And the last thing he remembered thinking was that God was justly punishing him for having been so weak for so long.

Fortunately for Diego, Lopez wasn't dead, although he regretted that briefly. No, he needed Lopez, needed his house, needed his contacts, needed his friends in high places. Primarily, he needed the money Lopez provided. How lucky for him to have been coming out of that bordello those many years ago, and at just the right time to see Lopez's little . . . error in judgment.

The fact that he'd told Lopez that the man he'd accidentally killed had been a high government official was a bit of quick thinking, though, he thought as he lifted Lopez from the floor and dragged him over to the long leather sofa.

With little difficulty, he arranged Lopez on the couch, face turned away from the door. There. That was good. It would fool the servants long enough, in much the same way as he had fooled Lopez all those years ago.

Lopez's target that night hadn't been some government official, just another patron of the house. And Lopez hadn't killed him. A wound to the scalp, that was all. Oh, the man had been unconscious, and there had been plenty of blood—enough to cover his face, hide his features, which Lopez had been loath to look upon anyway—but Diego had been certain that the gentleman in question would come around on his own in an hour or two.

In fact, once he'd got Lopez safely away from the scene of the crime, he'd gone back, just to make sure. Either that, or get rid of the body.

There had been no body to be found. Apparently, the man in question had simply gotten up and walked away.

Diego had thought it was a wonderful joke. And then, once he had thought about it further, he realized it was a wonderful opportunity.

He took advantage of it.

He slipped out of the study, only to run into the cook, about to knock on the door.

He put a finger to his lips and whispered, "Señor Lopez is taking a short siesta before dinner. He was very tired." He stepped aside to let her see the body on the sofa, to let her see Lopez's ribs gently rising and falling, and then he softly closed the door.

"I shall be in for dinner in a few minutes, Rosa," he said in his most charming voice. "I have a few things to attend to upstairs, first."

The cook nodded and smiled, dimples sinking into her chubby cheeks. Curtsying, she left him for the kitchen.

He started up the staircase, and stopped before the room with the armed guard outside. Really, it was just too simple!

"The ladies, they are comfortable?" he asked.

"Sí, señor," the guard replied curtly. There was a ring

of keys clipped to his belt, and Diego had a very good idea that the door was locked.

He smiled. This would be easy. Of course, there could be no noise, nothing to arouse suspicion. It would have to be quick, as well. There was a knife in his pocket, although he'd prefer to strangle them. Perhaps with his hands, perhaps with a pillow.

No, he couldn't give one the time to scream while he killed the other. Perhaps he could knock one out while he targeted the other with his blade.

Well, he would play it by ear, so to speak. He was adaptable.

He couldn't wait to see Lopez's face when he walked in to find his prizes, his excuses, dead. He had a feeling Lopez would never bother him again with this nonsense about closing the auction for good.

"Open the door," he said. "I have a message to convey, from Señor Lopez."

Surprisingly, the guard didn't give him any argument. He simply took the ring from his belt, sorted through the keys for a moment, picked one, and turned it in the lock.

"Call out to me when you wish to leave," the guard said.

Diego nodded. *"Gracias, amigo."*

He entered.

The room was a large one, and fit for a visiting dignitary. Much nicer than the one he had been given, he thought in irritation. It was lavishly furnished, with a massive bed, dressing table, bureau, and chifforobe, a table with four chairs, lavish lace curtains, and a huge fireplace.

But no women.

No women anyplace!

In desperation, Diego even peered under the rumpled bed and looked in the chifforobe.

What he found, however, was a rope of sorts, made

from knotted sheets, dangling out the window and se-
cured by the leg of that heavy table.

When he leaned out the window into the darkness,
there was no movement to be seen.

"*¡Mierda!*" he snarled, and stomped back to the door.
"Let me out!" he shouted. "Let me out, you idiot!"

17

After a long, careful lope, Garner and Hobie finally arrived in Galgo at about eight in the evening. Galgo was a poor excuse for a town, Garner thought, but he'd seen worse. At least Galgo had what appeared to be one decent hotel, and an equally decent livery. Probably for those once-a-year visitors, he thought bitterly. They came only once a year, for the auction. He'd like to get his hands on the organizers.

And if his luck held out, he would.

He and Hobie visited the livery first, and found it practically empty. It seemed that few of the locals used it. It had a large yard for parking carriages and such, and roomy box stalls on the inside.

"If you gentlemen had ridden in here one hour later," said the Mexican hostler, "I would have been closed for the season. But I will stay open for you." A middle-sized, mustachioed man who spoke perfect English, he ran an appreciative eye over Faro and Fly. "You have most handsome mounts."

"Thanks," replied Garner flatly. "Hobie?"

"Yup, I know," Hobie said, and led their horses to the two nearest boxes. He began to strip them of tack.

Garner leaned back against a post. "We missed the auction, I suppose," he said, adapting an air of resignation.

The stable man stared at them, studying them for a moment, then seemed to relax. "It is all over with. Everyone is gone, except the consignors." He winked. "They will get their pay tomorrow, and then, Señor, I advise you to stay indoors. It is always a wild bunch. And a wild bunch with money in their pockets . . . well, you know."

"Sure do," Garner replied.

From the stalls, Hobie called, "Dang! Did we miss the whole thing?"

And when Garner nodded, Hobie took off his hat and smacked his thigh with it. "Gosh-darn it, anyhow! I was countin' on findin' me a . . . Say, mister, whereabouts they hold this sale, anyhow? Mebbe they got some leftovers I could take a look at?"

Garner held back a smile. Smart kid.

The stable man studied on this for a moment. "Usually the *patrón* has one or two that do not sell. But I warn you, they are usually most unattractive. Or unmannered."

"I can whup some manners into her," Hobie said with the confidence of youth. "And it don't much matter what she looks like. Reckon I can do her with a bag over her head if I gotta. Just as long as she knows how to cook and clean up and spread her legs, that's all I care about."

Garner bit his lip. It was a good thing the stable man's attention was on Hobie. The kid was getting to be about as convincing a liar as Garner. At least, when it mattered.

Garner decided to help. He shook his head. "You got a one-track mind, kid," he said, sober as a judge. To the stable man, he added, "I keep telling him he can just rent one when he gets the urge."

"Not out in a line shack in the middle of winter!"

Hobie argued, and quite believably, too. "You never been out there all by your lonesome for months and months. Heck, the cows start to look good to a man after a while!"

Garner just shrugged. "All right, all right. I'm not gonna have this damned argument with you again. Do what you want. No skin off my back."

Hobie gave a satisfied smirk. "Whereabouts is it, mister?" he asked. "Could we make it tonight?"

Garner opened his mouth to add a pithy comment, but Hobie snapped, "I wanna get out there and pick over the leftovers before somebody else gets him an idea to do the same thing, all right?"

Garner held up both hands. "You win, kid. But I got a feeling you're gonna end up with a real dog on your hands."

The stable man pursed his lips for a moment, as if deep in thought. He stroked his mustache. Then, miraculously, he said, "I do not suppose it would do any harm. It is only a half hour's jog from here. I will make you a map. And when you come back, you can settle your own horses in. I am going home to get my dinner."

Garner flipped him a coin. "Enough for overnight?" he asked.

In the light of a lantern, the stable man peered at the coin, then nodded. "Enough. But only for one night. Tomorrow is the same again, if you are not gone before noon."

"Sounds fair," said Garner with a nod, even though the coin he'd tossed over had been a five-dollar gold piece. The stable man was a goddamn highway robber!

"Guess you'd best throw those saddles back on, kid," Garner added, and then turned to the stable man, who was busy drawing a map on the back of an old receipt. "Who do we ask for when we get out there?"

The stable man handed over the paper. "It says here," he replied.

"Don Carlos Lopez," Garner read, realizing as he said the words that this was Teach's "friend," the man to whom he'd sold his prize bull.

Some friend.

Startled, Hobie quickly looked up, but swiftly recovered. He tightened Fly's cinch. "Good," he said. "We can probably be back in an hour and a half. Hope the hotel's still servin' dinner. I could eat me a bear."

"If you should happen to make a purchase, my friend," said the stable man, heading toward the door, "you can leave her here for the night." He pointed toward a dark corner of the barn. "Most do."

And with that, he left.

Hobie started to speak, but Garner held up a finger to his lips, warning him that the stable man might be lingering outside, and picked up the lantern. He sauntered over toward the dark corner. "Sounds like a good idea, kid," he said as the lantern's light flooded the previously dark space. The wall was lined with manacles.

He ground his teeth angrily. Then, in a calm voice, he said, "Yup. Best leave her here where she can't go running off anywhere. Or keep the whole hotel awake all night."

Hobie led the horses out of their boxes, and only then did he see the manacles Garner was staring at.

He swallowed hard, but all he said was, "Yup."

The women had done the smartest thing they could, under the circumstances. They had climbed down their homemade "rope" quietly, and at dusk, when everyone had gone inside for dinner. Mary had noticed before that the hacienda was like some sort of feudal fortress. No walls, of course, at least, none that were complete, although she could see the remains of some that were ten feet tall, with niches cut along the top and middle. To

shoot from, she supposed. She also supposed that whoever was doing the shooting was doing it at Apaches.

But most of the wall was gone now, in these milder
times, gone to build the barns, of which there were three;
gone to build the smithy, the little harness shop, the
smokehouse, the workers' cottages, and more. She hadn't
seen very many workers or servants, though. Perhaps the
owner of this place, that man she had talked to, had sent
most of them away during the sale.

It had seemed the most likely thing to her.

At any rate, they shinnied down the rope with no problem, then moved quietly from shadow to shadow until
they reached the first barn. They were lucky. It was filled
with horses—not weanlings or yearlings, but riding
stock.

She saddled the first one she saw; Becky saddled another. Mary once again crept outside, just long enough to
fill four canteens with water. She tossed them inside to
Becky, and then made a dash to the smokehouse. They'd
need food.

Except that on her way, she had to pass what she assumed, by the bloody shirt of the man sitting before it,
lighting a cigarette, was the slaughterhouse. She waited
until he was intent on lighting his smoke, then tiptoed
past and out of sight.

At last she reached the smokehouse, and pulled down
a small ham and a turkey, then stole back the way she had
come. The man was still sitting there, smoking, but this
time he was intent on staring toward the horizon, at the
last rays of the sun.

For the second time, she made it past him unseen.

Becky took charge of the turkey, and Mary slipped the
ham into her saddlebag. She also noted that Becky had
filled her pockets before they climbed down from their
second-floor prison. She'd put all sorts of unexpected

treasures in Mary's saddlebag: a silver comb and brush, a tiny decorative pillow, edged in lace, and other things.

Mary looked up at Becky. It was really quite unexpected, not to mention odd. She whispered, "Why?"

Becky smiled sheepishly. "I thought they might help. You know, a lady like to look her best when she's . . . when she's in a family way."

Both Mary's brows shot up. "How? How did you know?"

"Lots of things," Becky said as she mounted the gray she'd picked out. "Like, you're beginnin' to show a little. And that what with all the hell we been through, you just keep lookin' prettier. You was in a family way before you was took, wasn't you?"

Mary climbed up on her bay. "Yes," she said softly.

Becky nodded. "Been thinking about it. Been thinkin' that it's why you didn't fight 'em so much when they . . . you know. You was afraid for the baby."

The child was certainly more intelligent than Mary had given her credit for. In the future, she told herself, she mustn't be so quick to judge.

But now the hardest part was ahead of them. It was dark outside by this time, and that would help shield them. It would not, however, make it easier to travel, particularly since they did not know the territory.

At least Mary knew which way was north, and she intended that they head there as quickly as they could. If nothing happened, if one of their horses didn't step in a gopher hole and break a leg, if they didn't get lost, if they didn't run into an unexpected mountain range, and if they weren't captured by a posse from the hacienda, they might make the border within two days.

She prayed they would.

"All right, Becky," she whispered. "It looks like nobody's missed us so far. We won't take the road. It's too dangerous. We'll have to go out through the desert, so be careful, honey. Now, follow me. And quietly."

"Mary?" Becky said wistfully, just as they were inching out the barn door and into the dark stable yard. "I wish I knew where they buried Mama."

Hobie rode along, just off Garner's right shoulder. They were nearly to the hacienda—or should be, according to Hobie's pocket watch. He'd just struck a match and had a peep at it, and gotten yelled at by Garner in the process.

"Why don't you just send up a flare while you're at it?" Garner had growled.

They had slowed to a jog in order to lessen the noise of travel, so Hobie figured that Garner was thinking the same thing he was. And now they had entered an area where the dusty lane was planted on each side with tall cyprus trees. They must be close.

Hobie twisted his head, like a hound dog who's caught just the tickle of a whiff of a scent.

"Hold up, Boss," he said.

Garner reined in Faro. "What?"

"Listen up," Hobie whispered. "Do you hear somethin'?"

He was certain he'd heard it—distant hoofbeats, galloping away. But they were gone now. He shook his head. "Sorry," he said. "I was certain sure . . ."

Apparently, Garner hadn't heard a thing, either. He just said, "Let's get to it," and urged Faro into a fast walk.

Hobie paced Fly to his speed.

"And just what are we gonna do once we get there?" he asked.

Garner shrugged. "Don't know."

"Oh, you're a lot of help," Hobie grumbled, and if Garner heard him, he didn't answer. That was a good thing, as far as Hobie was concerned. Heck, they might be riding into a hell-bent-for-leather gunfight! Just the two of them against Lord knows how many angry Mexicans.

But on the other hand . . .

He decided not to think about it until he had to.

Instead, he said, "You sure changed your tune on this deal."

Garner didn't reply.

"Well, first you didn't want to come at all, and then you did—"

"When I got that wire from you," Garner interjected. "HELP STOP COME QUICK STOP HOBIE," he quoted. "Or something like that."

Hobie noticed Garner didn't have to look at the telegram, which he knew was in Garner's pocket. It must have made some kind of impression, all right. He swallowed nervously.

"Now just what kind of a wire is that to go sending a man?" Garner went on. "Jesus, Hobie, you scared me half to death."

Now, Hobie knew this was a pretty big admission on Garner's part, and for just a second, he was kind of proud and happy.

"Should have ridden down there, all right, and whipped you good, pulling a fool stunt like that," Garner added, and all the Hobie's pride went squish.

"But you didn't," Hobie added meekly. "And you came."

"Only because you were acting so pitiful."

Hobie was losing control of the subject, and he knew it. He said, "Well, for as many times as you said she was dead, that they were all dead, and for as many times as you said it was a fool's errand we were goin' on, here you are. You must'a changed your mind."

"Nope," said Garner. "I still think she's likely dead or sold to South America someplace."

"Then why we ridin' out here?"

Garner pursed his lips for a second, his brow furrowing. "Because, Hobie, the whole thing just plain pisses me off. That's why."

It was enough for Hobie.

They started up into a soft jog again.

18

The first thing of which Lopez was aware was the pain.

The second, that he was lying on his side, on a leather sofa, and that he was facing the back of it.

The third, and most important, thing to come into his mind was *Diego*!

He sat up too fast, and had to wait a moment, elbows on his knees, hands holding his head. When he brought them away, there was blood on his fingers.

He rose, and gripping furniture to keep his balance, made his way to the door. He stepped into the doorway and bellowed, "Montoya! Where's Montoya?!"

Diego gave chase, as best he could, across the desert, and he was cursing with every beat of the horse's hooves.

Oh, this was a fine mess he'd gotten himself into. Cocky, that's what he'd gotten. Too damned cocky. He should not have struck Lopez. That was the first mistake. He should have reasoned with him, soothed him, promised him just one more year, anything. But the heft of all that gold in his hand, and the threat that there would be no more forthcoming—ever—had been too much for him. He had struck out with hardly a thought, and then marched upstairs to get rid of those two women. The way he saw it, they were the ones standing between him and a lifetime of easy money.

Well, he'd fix it. He'd catch those two *putas* and put them away, buried far out in the desert where no one would ever find them. Then he'd ride back and talk his way back into Lopez's graces.

He hardly noticed the scattered and drowsing cattle that he passed, except to curse the places where their tracks obscured the trail he was following.

"We'll allow no more kidnappings," he would say. "We will have rules again. I have been lax about that. Only girls sold to us by their parents or those who own their bond papers will be acceptable."

That should satisfy Lopez, at least temporarily. The rest, he would think of later. Right now, he had lost the trail and was searching for it again in the moonlight, zigzagging at a slow, high-stepping jog, casting his eyes out over the rough terrain.

Suddenly, his horse stepped into a hole of some sort, and nearly went down. As it was, the horse went to its knees and nearly jolted Diego from the saddle. He dismounted, once the animal had righted itself, and led it forward a few steps.

No harm, thank God.

It was a very good thing he had not been traveling faster.

He paused to take out a kerchief and wipe his forehead and calm himself. Also, to settle the horse.

That was when he saw it.

A small sage among many scattered throughout the landscape, a small sage with freshly broken twigs. He smiled, and led the horse the few steps over to it. He fingered the breaks.

There, on the stony, graveled ground, was the partial

imprint of a horseshoe. This was a hard place where few tracks were visible, but it was enough for Diego.

He mounted up again, and tried his best to study the distance. There was a small pass through the hills, perhaps five or six miles away. If he were those women, that was where he would head.

Of course, women were curious creatures, stupid and headstrong and unpredictable. Who knows what they would really do?

Diego shrugged. The pass, he supposed. If they did not go that way, then he would find them later, wandering the base of the mountain range. It was the only way through for many miles in either direction.

One way or another, he thought, he would find them. And when he found them, he would kill them.

How could his old friend Lopez explain that to the grieving husband?

Diego smiled and nudged his horse forward.

"Hold up," said Garner. Someone was coming down the road toward them, a rider in a hurry.

Hobie halted Fly. "You think we should get off this road, Boss?"

"Too late," Garner said.

The rider had already seen them, and was slowing his pace. He held up his hand in a greeting.

"Be ready, Hobie," Garner whispered.

From the corner of his eye, Garner saw Hobie nod in the affirmative.

The approaching rider had slowed to a jog, and then a walk. He stopped a few feet away. From what Garner could see by the moonlight, this was one tough hombre. However, he smiled at them.

"Americans?" he asked.

"Yup," said Garner, his hands relaxed, ready to go for his gun if need be.

"Excuse me," said the man. "I am Raul Montoya. I work for Don Carlos Ruiz Lopez. Perhaps you have heard of him?"

"We have," said Hobie. "Fact is, we're on our way to see him now."

Shut up, kid, Garner thought, and quickly broke in. "We're headed the right way, aren't we?"

Montoya nodded. "You will be there in less than ten minutes, Señors. And you have not given your names."

"Sorry," Garner answered before Hobie had a chance to. He'd done a damn fine job of lying back there in town, but Garner wasn't going to let him press his luck. "I'm Sam Jones from over New Mexico way." He jabbed a thumb toward Hobie. "And this here's my partner, Teddy White. Guess we're too late for the auction."

Montoya seemed to relax a little. "You are. Have you come from town?"

"Straight from it," said Hobie before Garner could.

Montoya nodded. "Have you seen two women on this road? Or a man?"

Garner shook his head. "Ain't seen nothin' but a couple of coyotes. You missin' folks?"

Montoya shrugged. "It is of no matter. *Gracias, amigos.*" And with that, he tipped his hat and galloped past them, toward town.

"Now, what the heck was that all about?" Hobie asked.

"I think maybe a couple of the gals hightailed it," Garner said.

"Let's hope it's a couple of ours," Hobie mumbled as they swung into a soft jog.

But Garner hadn't liked the looks of that Montoya in the least. He figured that if those gals were on the desert and Montoya caught up with them, they wouldn't last thirty seconds.

"Let's hope it's not," he replied.

• • •

Lopez had been told about the women's absence immediately after he'd called for Montoya, and had been advised
of Diego's hasty departure a few moments before Montoya arrived.

While Montoya was saddling his horse to ride out in
pursuit of Diego, and while the cook bandaged his head,
Lopez tried to gather his thoughts.

He wasn't having much luck.

Everything was muzzy. Just when he decided what it
was that he would do, the idea fled from his head just as
if it had trickled out his ear.

He'd been through this process of thinking and forgetting at least three times—that he remembered, that is—
and asked the cook, "Just how hard was I hit?"

"Patrón," Rosa said softly, her eyes filled with the
worry that comes with a lifetime of loyalty, "I think we
had best send to town, for the doctor."

"Nonsense," he answered, although he knew she was
probably right. When he looked up from his lap and held
his hand before him, he saw two blurry images instead of
a single distinct one.

He had always prided himself on his eyesight, on the
clarity of his vision. It must be something inside his head.
It hurt so much!

Rosa helped him stand up and walk to the door, where
he balanced himself on the frame. "All right, Rosa," he
said. "Send for him. But first, help me out to the chapel ."

"You must go up to bed," she said.

"No," Lopez replied firmly. His head pounded worse
with every moment, every movement. He thought that
perhaps trying to navigate the staircase might make it ex-
plode. "The chapel. It is closer, and I wish to pray."

She gave him no more argument. She never had, not in
all these years, not when the auctions started, not even
about the rowdy men that came to them. And she had
never, so far as he knew, breathed a hint of any of it to his

beloved wife and daughters. Perhaps she was ashamed for him.

Someone certainly should be.

As she helped him move falteringly out the door and traverse the few steps to the little private chapel, all Lopez could whisper was, *"Gracias, Rosa. Muchas gracias."*

She helped him to one of the two wrought-iron benches, and as he settled down, he saw her cross herself in the dim light from the doorway, light that was beginning to hurt his eyes, to burn into them terribly.

"I will light a lamp for you, *Patrón,*" she said. Even her soft words came to him like thunder.

To hush her, he held a shaky finger to his lips. "No light," he breathed. "And close the door behind you."

Wordlessly, accompanied only by the soft click of the door and the passage from light into darkness, she left.

There was no local priest to take his confession. Maybe in the old days there might have been, but Galgo had shrunk greatly in importance, giving its sea trade to larger, safer ports, and the population had gone where the trade was. Even the priest had gone along with them.

Considering that he was now the sole moneymaking enterprise in Galgo, outside of what business the cantinas and dry-goods store and the like brought to their owners, he did not blame the priest.

He had helped make Galgo what it was. He had been the devil's instrument, Diego's instrument.

He only realized that he had thudded to the floor because of the pain it caused, the pain that jolted through his head like a thousand bolts of lightning.

"Forgive me, Father, for I have sinned," were the last words that escaped him as he fled into darkness, into the unknowable.

• • •

At the Tres Lobos Cantina, Chambers was sitting back, slowly nursing a whiskey. He'd given up looking for Smeed. And if the runty little bastard didn't show up in the morning to collect his half of the money? Well, tough.

Montoya usually rode into town and opened up shop at around nine. When he did, Chambers would be first in line with his hand out, palm open.

Chambers hoped Smeed had really tied one on this time. Or maybe gotten himself into another fight. Either one would keep him sleeping—or unconscious—till noon, and Chambers could be long gone by then. He'd go so far and so wide that Smeed would never find him.

Of course, there was that sonofabitch he'd hit today. It still made him mad, just thinking about it. Not that the bullet had hit somebody, of course, but that he'd missed his original target.

Well, he'd shot them up good enough that they must have had to slow down. And besides, he'd been too far away from them to see, even if he hadn't slid and skittered down the backside of that hill like the devil himself was on his tail.

No, they couldn't pin that one on him.

He smiled and took another sip of whiskey.

Things were looking up.

19

Montoya walked through the cantina's batwing doors and quickly took in the scenery. He walked directly over to Chambers's table.

When Chambers saw him, the chair upon which he had been tilted back came upright in a hurry, the two front legs hitting the tiled floor like gunshots. Montoya gave a tiny jump—which was lost on Chambers—and for just a moment, all conversation in the little bar stopped, but just as quickly started up again.

Chambers scrambled to his feet. He even took off his hat, the bastard.

"You come into town this early to pay us, Mr. Montoya?" Chambers said.

"No," Montoya said. He knew that this one was partnered with Smeed, whose remains were currently being enjoyed by the livestock. He also knew that Lopez would probably want this one disposed of in the same manner.

But Montoya had a better idea. Chambers could perhaps serve him better in another way.

He could always kill him later.

Montoya pulled up a chair and motioned Chambers down again.

"I am looking for Diego Mondragon," he said, leaning close to Chambers's eager ear. "Have you seen him this night?"

"Ain't seen nobody," Chambers said with a shrug. "Just come into town myself. Been out . . . um, sight-seein'."

"Would you know him if you were to see him?" Montoya asked.

"Sorry, no," Chambers replied. He scratched at his belly. "You sure you can't pay me tonight? I'd . . . that is, me and my partner, we'd like to cut out of town real early in the mornin'. A feller I talked to said you made out real good on them gals we brought you."

Montoya almost smiled. Chambers would get his wish—the one about "cutting out"—although not precisely in the manner he had intended.

Montoya said, "Perhaps tonight, if you can do a little job for me."

Chambers leaned across the table. "Somethin' extra in it for me?"

Montoya allowed his hidden smile to leak out a little. "Oh, yes, something extra. Something quite amazing."

"I'm your man," Chambers said.

Montoya nodded. *"Bueno,"* he said. "I want you to find Diego Mondragon. He is tall and slim, a handsome man. He rides a black stud horse, a tall, fancy one, and has silver conchos on his saddle skirts and *tapaderas*. You could see him from a mile away with this moon. I think he is heading north."

"Sure," Chambers said. "What you want I should do with him once I find him?"

Montoya leaned back in his chair and began to roll a cigarette. "I want you to kill him, and bring his body back to the home of Señor Lopez."

Chambers didn't even flinch. Montoya had guessed that he wouldn't.

"All right, sure," Chambers said. "Whatever you say. And about my partner . . ."

"Four hundred in gold is what we will pay for Diego's body," Montoya replied, pulling a figure from the air. "However you wish this reward to be split is up to you."

Chambers nodded greedily. "Which way'd he head out, and when'd he ride off?"

"He left the hacienda about thirty, maybe forty minutes ago," Montoya said, lighting his smoke. A pretty girl slid a warm *cerveza* in front of him, and he said, "*Gracias,* Carmelina."

To Chambers, he continued. "He did not come to town on the road. I did not catch him on my way in, and no one I have talked to so far has seen anyone of his description. So he must have ridden north, over the desert."

"Well, that makes it easy," Chambers said. He tossed back the last of his whiskey and stood up. "They's only the one pass anybody can go through to come south or go north around here. I'll get your feller for you."

He started to leave, then turned back to Montoya. "How much them three gals of ours bring, anyhow?"

Montoya shrugged. "Sorry, *compadre,* I need to consult my books." He held up his hands, empty save for a cigarette smoldering in the left one. "You will find out when you come to the house. Perhaps we can pay you then, make an exception."

Chambers left, the doors swinging behind him. Montoya sipped at his beer.

"Yes, my friend, you will find out," he said softly over the clatter of clicking heels and the arguing and chatter and guitar music in the background. "You will find out. And you know, some of it I think you are not going to like so very much."

He smiled wide, took another slug of his beer, then

went outside to take a leisurely ride back to the house to cool out his mount. Then he would check on Lopez, then perhaps do some scouting for tracks. He hadn't thought to do so before. He'd just come straight into town.

It wasn't like him, not to think things through before he acted. That's how worried about Lopez he'd been. That wound hadn't looked good to him. So much blood! Of course, he knew there was always much blood with a scalp wound, but this one had looked more . . . indented.

On second thought, he mused as he rode the sweaty bay gelding up Galgo's excuse for a main street, he should stop at the doctor's house and take him along, willing or unwilling.

Yes, that would be best. This early in the evening, perhaps Dr. Ricardo would not be so drunk.

A short distance north of the pass, Will was still clearing his head from the laudanum daze. He sat up again, poked at the fire with his good arm, and idly studied the Captain.

It had been too good to last, that little remission. The man who lay before him, barely conscious, wasn't the Captain of that morning, and in more ways than one. Something about this last episode—whether it was Will getting himself shot by that anonymous assassin, or the Captain wrenching his back again when they were so close to Galgo and possibly Mary—had taken the heart right out of him.

Well, come to think of it, he didn't imagine the Captain would be brokenhearted about him getting shot up. It was Mary—and Mary alone—that had laid the Captain's mind so low.

He thought he saw the Captain's hand moving, feeling for the laudanum bottle again, and painfully, he leaned forward.

"No, you don't," he said through gritted teeth, and

snatched up the bottle before the Captain's groping fingers could find it. Will held the bottle up in a direct line with the fire and checked its level. "There's only enough left for two doses, Captain," he said. "I can go without, but this has got to last you until Garner and Hobie get back."

And then he thought, if they do come back. Damn it, anyway!

The Captain muttered something under his breath.

"What was that?" Will asked. It was a clear night. He could see silvery desert for at least thirty yards in every direction.

"Mary, Mary," repeated the Captain, and brought his arm up over his face.

"It's the poppy juice," Will said softly, as much to cover his embarrassment as the Captain's. Cavalry officers, even ex-cavalry officers, were supposed to be tough. Like their sergeants. "It's just that old poppy juice talkin'," he said. "Garner's a good man, and that Hobie kid's no slouch, either. If somebody else had to go in besides us, I'm glad it was them."

That was the honest truth.

Just as Garner and Hobie came to the part of the road that turned where the long, private drive opened up into a ranch yard, a rider came barreling toward them.

Both he and Hobie reined their mounts to the side, and a good thing, too, because even then, Hobie just missed getting knocked off his horse. The rider didn't slow, just raced past them and into the darkness. Garner could hear his hoofbeats fade into the distance.

"Cripes!" said Hobie, and felt both himself and Fly— to see if they were all there, Garner guessed. "Somethin's sure goin' on up at the house, too."

He was right. All the lights were ablaze, and there were men running all over the place.

Well, hell. This took care of any stealthy maneuvers that Garner might have come up with. He supposed the only thing to do was ride right up to the door, big as life. Gently, he reached down his thigh to his Colt. He clicked it over to let the hammer cover a loaded chamber.

"Best be ready, Hobie," he said.

Hobie was already doing the same. "Right, Boss. You got anything in mind?"

"Let's just ride on up like we own the place," Garner said hopefully.

They started forward again, riding directly into the center of a pack of milling hands. Their posture nearly allowed them to get away with it, too.

And then somebody recognized them as strangers. A big Mexican grabbed Garner's reins, and he snatched them back automatically. Which caused the big Mexican to yank him down off his horse.

Garner slugged him one time, square in the jaw, and the Mexican went down at just about the time six or seven more came at him.

Fortunately—and at last—Garner had the sense to jump back a couple of feet and hold up his hands. "Hold it!" he shouted. "Whoa up, boys!"

The first Mexican that had come at him was on his feet again, and he said something rapidly in Spanish that halted the others. Hobie was off his horse, too, but separated from Garner by about fifteen feet and nearly as many men.

"Who are you and what do you want here?" the man asked in heavily accented English.

"We've come to see Señor Lopez," Garner boomed out. "On business."

"How do we know you were not here earlier?" another voice asked, this one issuing from a wiry vaquero with a face like an axe. His hand was on the butt of his pistol.

Garner held up his hands again. "Look, we just rode in

from town. You could ask the fellow at the stable. I don't know what's going on here, but—"

"*El Patrón,* he has been attacked!" said a third man. Garner didn't see him.

"Señor Mondragon did it," snapped the first Mexican. "Montoya said so."

"Then why you pull him off his horse, Miguel?" demanded the wiry one.

"Hold it!" Garner said, and amazingly, everybody did. "You boys telling me that somebody shot Lopez?"

The big man shook his head. "How you Americans say? Buffalo. He was buffaloed, no?"

"Hit upside the head?" Garner asked.

All the Mexicans nodded.

"Bad," said the big man. He swept off his sombrero reverently. "Rosa, she sends for Dr. Ricardo." Several men behind him crossed themselves.

"It was those women," grumbled an unseen voice, in Spanish. Garner understood, but pretended he didn't.

"Sorry, friend," Garner said, brow furrowing. "Is there anything my friend and I can do?" He hoped that if that unseen ranch hand spoke again, he'd say more about these women, and that he'd talk awful slow.

"*De nada,*" said the big Mexican, and slid his sombrero back on his head. "There is nothing."

"Except to pray, Miguel," said another voice, softly.

A chorus of "*Sí, Sí*" echoed softly through the throng.

Once again, that voice sounded in Spanish. "It was those women, I tell you. Why did Señor Lopez keep them back in the first place?"

Garner stared straight at Miguel, the big man, and said, "Terrible shame."

He thought he'd gotten the gist of what had been said. Apparently, these two women that had taken off—the two that the man on the road had asked about—had been held back from the auction. He just wished that somebody would mention names.

Not to mention a few directions.

Just then, the big hacienda's front door opened and a weeping women, middle-aged and round-hipped, staggered out, holding her apron up over her face.

"Rosa!" one of the men shouted.

As she went down to her knees, still weeping, the whole mob of Mexicans moved rapidly toward her. Garner was swept along. He caught a glimpse of Hobie out of the corner of his eye. He had managed to avoid being caught in the throng, and was grabbing for Faro's reins.

Miguel reached the woman first, and bent down to her. Garner couldn't hear a thing. And then Miguel stood up. He removed his sombrero once again, but this time very slowly.

He held up a hand, and the mob fell silent.

"Don Carlos Ruiz Lopez is dead," Miguel announced solemnly.

"Murdered!" cried another angry voice.

Good, thought Garner, although his face was filled with nothing but pity.

From the ground, Rosa wailed in Spanish, "Why did the *Patrón* not sell those *putas* with the rest? It is their fault, that Teach woman and the other. They should never have run away."

Even if Garner had missed most of what she said—which he did, because it was full of weeping and sniffling—he still would have caught the name Teach. And "run away."

He nearly smiled.

He didn't, though. To Miguel, he said, "This fellow that murdered Lopez. You say he took off?"

Miguel nodded his shaggy head, still hatless.

"Which way'd he go?"

"I do not know, Señor," he replied ruefully. "If I did,"

he added, his face clouding, then turning toward a snarl, "I would—"

"I know," said the wiry fellow. "I saw him, Miguel. I could not catch Montoya before he left for town, but I saw where this murdering Diego Mondragon went."

"Where?" demanded Miguel.

The wiry Mexican's hand thrust out. His finger pointed. "North. To the pass."

Garner started backing up. Nobody noticed. But as he quietly joined Hobie and took Faro's reins, he heard Miguel say, "*El Patrón*, his death will not go unavenged, Rosa."

As Garner mounted, he heard Miguel cry. "Ride, vaqueros!"

"Let's get out of here and beat the crowd," Garner muttered to Hobie as he nudged Faro into a lope. The horses were tired. They'd had an awfully long day. But it would just have to be a little longer.

Hobie and the buckskin Fly paced him, step for step.

"Excuse me for askin'," Hobie shouted as they galloped out, over the silvery desert, "but what do we want with this Diego feller?"

They were now traveling at a full gallop, and the night wind burned Garner's cheeks and threatened to take his hat. He cupped a hand to his mouth and shouted back, "We want him because he's chasing Teach's wife!"

He wasn't quite certain what it was that Hobie shouted back at him—he was too busy reining around a moon-shadowed cactus—but it sounded like, "Hot damn!"

20

Mary had succeeded in thinking like her Sam, now, without noting it. She had to, if she wanted to live.

She'd glimpsed the rider behind them a few minutes ago, and had fallen back briefly to quirt Becky's lagging mount. The roan rocketed ahead, much to Becky's consternation—at least, she shouted something distinctly unfeminine once she regained her seat—and now, they were almost at the pass.

Mary knew that if she could see the rider behind them, he could surely see them.

She'd briefly considered stopping and shooing the horses on and hoping he'd pass by, but she quickly came to the conclusion that it would never work. First, what was her insurance that the horses they'd stolen would continue to run on? And even if they did, even if they made it all the way to the American border, she and Becky would be two women in the desert, without food or water.

If they hadn't already expired by the time that man

came back, looking for them, he would surely find them and drag them back to that horrible place.

Or worse.

They hadn't a single weapon between them. Oh, Mary had thought of it while they were furtively saddling the horses. She'd actually looked for a gun, even a knife, but the only weapon in the stable had been a pitchfork and a couple of bullwhips.

She glanced back again.

This time, she didn't see the man. But she knew that didn't mean he wasn't back there.

She slowed her mount again and to Becky, shouted, "Hurry, blast you!"

She quirted Becky's roan again, and they bolted through the beginning of the long pass.

Diego Mondragon was growing weary of these damnable women.

He had chosen his mount, Brio, for looks rather than speed. After all, how often did one need to race around when one's interests lay elsewhere? In card games and women and fine wines, for instance.

Brio was handsome and stylish, a high-stepping Paso Fino who impressed even those who knew little about horses. But he was not fast.

Diego had caught sight of the women exactly once, and then lost them again. Perhaps they had sprinted ahead. Perhaps the moon was not as bright as it had been before. But he suspected the former. The moon was still high and huge, the sky perfectly clear.

As he neared the dip in the line of shallow hills that marked the pass, it occurred to him that he would most likely have to apologize to Lopez. The thought rankled, but it still had to be done.

He had been rash, he would say. He would return half the money currently weighing heavy in his saddlebags.

He would tell Lopez that the women had escaped, but were now dead and no more worry to him. Or anyone else, for that matter.

And he would remind Lopez that he, Diego Mondragon, was in charge.

He dug his spurs into Brio's flanks once more. The horse tried to bolt ahead, but there was little increase in speed.

"Pathetic," Diego muttered, but didn't hear his own voice.

It was lost in the wind.

Milt Chambers, although still a little drunk, was making good time toward the pass when he saw—or thought he saw—two riders cutting across the plain. Just tiny specks, but to his sniper's eye, visible.

He reined in his horse just long enough to pull out his spyglass and confirm that he hadn't gone loco. That they weren't a couple of pronghorns out for a midnight gallop. And that he wasn't *that* drunk.

There they were, two men on horseback, going lickety-split right toward the place he was headed—the break in the hills.

He couldn't make out anything more than that, but it was enough. He'd be damned if he'd let anybody else pick up that four-hundred-dollar reward!

He dug his heels into the horse and bent low and forward, into the wind.

It had just better not be that sonofabitching Smeed with a new partner, that was all he had to say.

The Captain had dozed off again, although Will noted that he sure seemed a lot less fuddled than he had earlier in the evening. Of course, Will himself was in a lot more pain, but he didn't take a sip from that laudanum bottle, didn't even consider it. He knew the Captain was hurting, too, and probably a lot worse than he was.

If Garner and Hobie didn't get back pretty soon, he and the Captain were going to be in a real fix, all right. Will figured about a day was all the Captain could make that last little bit of poppy juice last. And Garner had best keep his word about bringing that wagon and some more laudanum, too.

Will leaned carefully back against a rock and let his eyes close to slits. He couldn't go to sleep. Someone had to keep watch. Besides, he didn't think he could sleep anyhow, not with his hurt shoulder hammering at him.

He thought about Bess and the boys, thought about Shorty and Butter Pie dozing a few yards away, thought about the ranch back home, and wondered if the hands were getting over to the Captain's place every day to water and feed the stock.

He wondered about his own stock.

But mostly, he wondered why he just hadn't gone off with that posse in the first place. Now that he knew Hobie had been with them, why, they could have lit out, the two of them! They would have made a lot better time than he had coming down late, towing the Captain like a china teacup. He and Hobie probably would have caught up with those kidnapping sonsofbitches on the desert, before they ever got all the way to Galgo, before they even crossed the border!

But then, there was Bess telling him no, looking stern but worried, and saying, "Don't be a fool, Will Thurlow. They've got a United States marshal leading them! What help could you possibly be?"

But then, Bess hadn't known that U.S. Marshal Ned Smallie would turn out to be more useless than tits on a boar hog.

He hadn't, either.

Hindsight, all hindsight.

His eyes fluttered despite the pain. He sat up all the way once more, and slowly reached for another handful of the dry sticks that Hobie had hurriedly gathered for the fire that afternoon. Will stirred the fire, sending up a flurry of sparks toward the moon, and then, a little at a time, his teeth gritted, he eased back against the rock.

Once again, he let his eyes half-lid. His left hand was on his rifle's stock, for what little good it would do if he should need it. Just threaten and bellow, that was all he was good for, what with his right shoulder banged up. He doubted he could hit the side of a barn with a handful of beans with his left.

He grumbled beneath his breath: not words, just sounds. The kind, on the surface, that he'd make if one of the boys tried to wake him on a Sunday morning, when he was pretending to be asleep. This grumble was real, though, and distinctly filled with pain and helplessness.

Damn that sniper, anyway! Now, who would want to go and shoot him? He'd never even been to Mexico, and therefore couldn't have made any enemies.

It was stupid and senseless, that's what it was, and off and on he felt like he could strangle that bastard with his one good hand.

He probably could have, too.

That is, if he hadn't finally fallen asleep.

Garner spotted the signs again. Three horses, and recent.

They were on the right track, all right. He glanced over his shoulder, and could see no one. They had a good lead on the boys from the hacienda.

Frankly, he didn't give a good goddamn about this Diego Mondragon. The boys could have him. He wanted those women. Either that, or he wanted to chase them right into the arms of Teach and Will.

Hobie must have been thinking the same thing, because he shouted, "You figure Will and Captain Teach'll be able to defend themselves?"

Garner raised his hand, signaling Hobie to slow down. He eased up on Faro, too, and paused to run a hand along the bay's sweaty neck. "Sorry, boy," he whispered. "I promise, it's not much farther."

"I don't know," he said in answer to Hobie's query. He honestly didn't. He hoped Will was a fair-to-middlin' shot with his left hand. If those women did find Will and Teach, that is. If Will had let the fire die down, they might miss them entirely and keep on running.

Or they might see the fire, and swing wide around it.

He tried to think what he'd do if he was in their place, but it was hard. First, he couldn't imagine what it would be like to be a woman, particularly a woman that had gone through the ordeal that those two had most likely endured.

"These horses have about had it," Hobie said. They were down to a jog now, but it wasn't soft and it wasn't slow. Fly was as lathered up as Faro, but just as game, too. But Garner had noticed that Faro wasn't tugging at the bit anymore. He was willing, but he wasn't really enthusiastic about it.

"I know," Garner said. "We can swap horses with Will if the women don't see their fire and stop."

"And just who's gonna walk out Faro and Fly?" Hobie asked.

Garner signaled to slow up a little more. Thinking quickly, he said, "We can put 'em on ropes and Will can lunge them in circles, from the ground."

Hobie nodded. "Never thought of that."

And then, after a long silence, Hobie added, "I sure hope they see 'em. That Mrs. Teach sees their fire, I mean. I hope Will didn't let it go out. I reckon I left him enough wood to last the night, don't you?"

Garner grunted in the affirmative and glanced over his shoulder once more. Still no sign of that posse.

He said, "Let's move on back up to a lope, Hobie."

Mary and Becky stumbled out of the north end of the pass quite literally, with Becky's mount going down to its knees. Becky went sailing, and Mary quickly stopped and dismounted.

When Mary saw that Becky was moving and therefore not dead, she checked the roan, leading it forward a few feet. She bent to feel the leg carefully. It wasn't broken, she was certain, but the gelding was going to be useless for riding, and likely would remain so for months.

Swearing under her breath, she stripped tack from the roan and smacked it across the backside, sending it on. It limped away into the darkness as Mary bent to Becky.

"You all right?" she asked. "Did you break anything?"

Becky grimaced. "Landed on my hip," she said as Mary helped her to her feet. "I don't think anything's busted, though."

"Can you ride?"

"I reckon," Becky replied gamely. "It's just the getting on I'm not sure about."

Becky hobbled to Mary's mount with Mary's help, and at last managed to climb aboard. Mary mounted up behind her, searching the darkness for any trace of their pursuer.

"Head for . . ." Mary began, and then stopped and squinted ahead.

"Head for what?" Becky asked.

Mary's arm shot out. "There. Over there! Is that a fire?"

"I don't see one. I don't see anything but dark."

"Just go that way," Mary said with another imperative jab of her fingers to the north, and dug her heels into the horse.

It didn't occur to her that the men who had made that fire might be dangerous. It didn't occur to her that they might be slavers—or buyers—just come from that horrid place.

The only thought in her head—for she had come back into herself in the exact instant she saw that tiny speck of glow in the distance—was *Sam*.

21

Diego was halfway through the pass when his horse threw him.

He stood up slowly, feeling for broken bones or sprained muscles, and only after he was certain he was unharmed—and had not lost his weapons—did he check to see about Brio.

The horse was up, his ebony sides and neck covered with foam, his ribs heaving, his breathing labored. The long, luxurious, black mane and forelock that had captivated many a *señorita* hung tangled and damp and flecked with froth.

Diego led the horse forward a few yards, then pursed his lips. A little limping. Not serious, though, he thought.

Besides, it couldn't be serious, not now. It was too important. He had to catch those two bitches before it was too late, and he couldn't do it on foot.

He led Brio forward another couple of yards. Was it his imagination, or had the limping lessened?

He mounted again and gathered his reins. "You had better be all right, Brio, or I shall have to shoot you," he muttered under his breath, and urged the horse forward, into a fancy, high-stepping trot. The horse could move no other way.

The gait was uneven because of the limp, but Diego decided he could bear it. "Good fellow," he said, more to himself than the horse.

The gait, the fastest he could push the horse now, was even rougher by the time he came out of the north end of the pass. He was concentrating so much on keeping his seat that he was practically on it before he saw it: a saddle and blanket, the bridle carelessly tossed on top.

Diego's brow creased. He pulled up the grateful Brio. He scanned the distance, or at least, as much of it as he could see in the moonlight.

There! Was that movement? His pistol was halfway free of its holster before he realized it was a riderless horse, limping slowly through the brush.

Diego smiled.

Teach thought he was dreaming. He thought he was dreaming about camping on the desert miles south of the U.S. border, that someone had stolen away his Mary and that he was on their trail, and that he hurt, he hurt.

"Sam, Sam," said Mary in the dream, and she was weeping. "Oh, my Sam, my beautiful pirate."

And then, through the laudanum haze, he became aware that this wasn't a dream, not a phantasm or delusion. His Mary was there beside him, holding him, calling his name.

"Mary," he breathed happily. A single tear escaped his eye before he lapsed again into darkness.

The Captain lay senseless in his wife's arms, and Will still couldn't believe it. She was sitting right there, big as life in a fancy but rumpled mustard-colored dress, and he still had to rub at his eyes.

"Will, what's wrong with him?" she demanded.

The other gal, who had ridden in on the same horse with Mary, blinked and asked, "Is this your husband, Mary?" Then she turned to Will and asked, "Is he really her man?"

Will nodded curtly before he realized he was still clutching his rifle. Uselessly, but he was clutching it. He laid it down on the ground beside him and, in a shaking voice, said, "Mary, he got hurt. Right after you were took. But how did you get here? Where are those snakes that took you off? How did—?"

"You're hurt too, mister," interrupted the other female, who was just a child. She pointed at his bandaged shoulder. "You do that patchin' yourself?"

Will ignored the question. Mary was rocking her husband, and Will had to tell her, "Best not, Mary. Don't move him, all right? See, there's a slug lodged—"

The sound of a single shot cut Will off, midsentence.

Garner and Hobie heard it, too, even though they were only halfway up the pass. Without a glance passing between them, they both put heels to horseflesh and jumped ahead as one.

His horse tail flapping out from behind his hat, Milt Chambers, who was just about to enter the pass, heard it, too. Angrily, he lashed his mount ahead.

Somebody thought he'd just taken the reward for Diego Mondragon, but by God, the bastard wasn't going to live to claim it!

Will looked up sharply, and brought his Winchester to bear at the same time.

The figure clicked his tongue slowly. In a voice accented heavily in Spanish, the man said, "I would not try it, Señor. You appear to be using your weak hand, and trust me, I am very proficient with this firearm."

Just loud enough for him to hear, Mary whispered, "No, no, no . . ."

Slowly, Will lowered the rifle. He had no choice.

"Who are you?" he called.

The man began to walk forward, his face becoming a little clearer with every step.

"I have no quarrel with you, Señor," the voice said. "I simply wish to reclaim my property."

"There's nothing here belongs to you, mister," Will called. He could see that the man was tall—probably not as tall as he was, though—and lean and good-looking. Not old, not young, although he had a little gray at the temples. He looked, in fact, like a cardplaying dandy, or the Mexican version of one.

"You are mistaken, I think," the fellow said. "You have two things that belong to me."

He stopped about twenty feet back from the fire, and waved his gun at Mary. "You will stand up, please, Señora."

Mary didn't move.

"Who the hell are you?" Will repeated, this time virulently. "Who the hell are you to come in here and wave your side arm around?"

"Forgive me," said the man. "You may call me Diego, and I am the man to whom these two runaway wenches belong. I am here to reclaim them. With your permission or without."

"Without," growled Will. He wondered just how good this Diego was with a firearm. Would it be possible for Will to reach across and draw his gun? No, even if Diego was a lousy shot, he'd have time to get off three or four rounds before Will could even get his fingers on his pistol's grip.

For an instant, he wished his Bess was here with him.

She'd rip this fancy little pissant's head off and fry it for breakfast, and she wouldn't need a gun to do it.

Diego repeated, "Stand up."

Mary just stared at him. Will had never seen that particular expression, so full of hate and loathing and fear, on Mary's face before. He hoped to never see it again.

"All right," said Diego. "I will shoot you where you sit, then. But first," he added, twisting toward the other gal, "we will take care of you, no?"

The girl covered her eyes with her hands and shrank toward the ground, crying, "Mama, Mama!"

Diego shook his head—in disgust, Will was pretty sure—and cocked his pistol.

With a herculean effort born of long training and habit, Will ignored the pain and threw himself between the girl and the gunman, at the same time trying to reach around his belly for the holstered pistol.

He fell short, both with the effort to reach the girl and to grab his pistol. The shots sounded before he made either goal.

But the girl, the target, only jumped and peeked between her fingers, and Diego dropped his gun. A half second later, he went to his knees, then fell forward into the shadows on his face.

Shaking with pain, Will whispered, "God provides. By jing, He does!"

A few minutes later, Garner and Hobie walked up toward the fire, leading their horses and the black one, the one they'd found ground-tied farther out. Garner's rifle still swung easy in his hand.

Hobie didn't come into the fire's circle, just tipped his hat to the ladies and set off to continue walking the horses.

"Get that chestnut, too," Garner called as he nudged Diego's body with the nose of his rifle. "He looks like he's all in, and there's nobody tending to him." He knelt and checked for a pulse. There was none.

"Yeah," grumbled Hobie good-naturedly. "I got ten hands. No problem, Boss. No problem at all."

Diego was dead, all right, although Garner was annoyed that he wasn't the shot he used to be, regardless of how carefully he had sighted down on the back of Diego's head. But even though the bullet had come in low, it had still neatly separated Diego's spine at the neck.

But another bullet had taken Diego in the side.

Garner's brow furrowed and he scratched his neck.

"Everybody all right?" he asked as he walked up to the fire. He was pretty sure they were all still unharmed and breathing, but he wanted to hear it from them. "Who fired? Besides me, I mean."

"Where's the wagon?" Will asked.

Garner shook his head. "Dammit, Will, I can't do everything." And then he looked over at the older of the two women in camp, who was crouched over the unconscious Teach. She held Teach's pistol in her hand.

It could only be one person.

"Mrs. Teach, ma'am," he said, and tipped his hat.

She nodded her head. "And you are, sir?"

"This is Deputy U.S. Marshal King Garner, Mary," said Will for him. "And that young feller with the horses is Deputy U.S. Marshal Hobie Hobson. They came across the border to find you."

"Unofficially," Garner said, and shifted his weight from one boot to the other. Even, after years, the title of deputy U.S. marshal still embarrassed him. To cover it, he turned to the other woman, who he only then saw was just a girl. "Miss," he said, and thumbed his hat.

"Becky," she said shyly. "Becky Lowell, Marshal."

"Just call me Garner," he said. "You hurt?"

Becky shook her head.

"Then, would you mind giving Hobie a hand with the horses?" he asked.

"Sure, mister," she replied, her voice very small and very young.

He glanced into the darkness from which he and Hobie had come. Nothing yet. His attention turned to Mrs. Teach.

"Did you fire?" he asked.

She looked down at the gun, then tossed it away. So soft that he hardly heard it, she said, "Yes."

Garner nodded. "Good shot." He pointed toward the campfire and asked Will, "That coffee still hot? We're gonna have a whole bunch of boys thundering in here in a few minutes, and I'd like to rest my bones a mite before we start getting ready for 'em."

"It's hot," said Will, concern furrowing his brow. "What boys?"

Garner poured himself a cup of coffee and took a sip. It wasn't exactly hot, but it wasn't exactly cold, either.

"Long story," he replied.

"I got time," Will said.

22

After first spotting the distant campfire, Milt Chambers had turned around and retraced his tracks one hundred yards. Then he'd taken the same little cut up into the hills he'd used before.

He was presently once again up on top of the rock, his sweating horse tethered at the base of the pinnacle. Once again, he was sighting down on the pass below.

But where the hell was this Diego character, and why had those folks at the fire shot their guns off? He'd picked out two of those women he and Smeed had hauled down from the States, and he couldn't figure out what the heck they were doing there. Somebody'd have to be loony to take them back up into Arizona!

He moved the muzzle of his rifle just slightly, and settled his scope on the fat Swede's face. He found the other two men that had been with the Swede before, too, but he still hadn't found his previous target, old Hard to Kill.

The bastard.

He became aware of a rumbling down below and to

the south, and made himself relax and swing the sights in that direction.

In the shadows of the pass, he could barely make them out. But they were coming, all right. A whole mob of them.

He picked out a face he'd seen before. He didn't know the man's name, but he knew he worked for the same outfit Montoya did. Shit! What was wrong with that goddamn Montoya, anyhow, sending a whole passel of men out when he'd already sent Chambers?

Montoya should have known he'd sent the best already, should have known he didn't need to hedge his bets.

Chambers smiled. Well, if they were looking for Diego Mondragon down there, they weren't going to find him.

Of course, he hadn't searched the rest of the campfire site yet.

At this thought, he swung the rifle back down on the little group below.

What the hell?

Now both of the women were gone. Nowhere. Just vanished. And there was sure a fancy black horse tied to their picket line. He hadn't seen that before, and pounded a fist against his knee as punishment for his oversight.

He'd bet anything that was Diego's nag, the sonofabitch! But where was he?

He began sweeping the scope over the ground, rather than the faces.

There! He could see booted feet sticking out from behind a rock. Not enough to take a shot at, but at least it identified an extra body, which might be old Hard to Kill's or Diego Mondragon's.

Now, he might have gone ahead and taken a shot, even

if it was only at a boot, but just then Montoya's boys galloped under his roost and toward the distant fire.

He kept watching.

Muttering, "Here they come," Garner got to his feet.

He slowly walked around the fire, built larger now,
and toward the incoming riders, then stopped out in the
weeds, right over Diego Mondragon's body. The posse
reined in about five or six yards away from him.

"Howdy, fellers," Garner said, rolling a cigarette. "Believe we got your boy right here." He pointed down at the
ground.

While he backed off a couple of feet, then licked his
smoke and stuck it in his mouth, Manuel dismounted and
walked up. He had a good stare down at the body, then
spat on it.

"You have got him indeed," Manuel said. He almost
looked disappointed. Garner figured that he wouldn't
have wanted to be in Diego's shoes if this gang had
caught up with him first.

Manuel went back to his horse and brought a rope.
Garner didn't question him as he proceeded to tie Diego's
feet to it, then tie the other end to his saddle horn. He just
lit his smoke.

"You boys going back to the old hacienda tonight?" he
asked, as if he were going to add that it was late, and why
didn't they stay till morning.

But Manuel said, "We go, Señor, and we take this
piece of dog's vomit with us." He mounted and evened
his reins. "You can keep his horse," he said in what
seemed an afterthought. "Or you could shoot it," he
added with a shrug.

Manuel reined away, and Garner stood there and
smoked that cigarette until the last one of those Mexicans
had trotted out of sight and into the night, hooting and
hollering and dragging Diego Mondragon behind them.

And then he stood there a little longer.

At last he turned toward Hobie, back at the fire, and said, "All right. You can go get them now. We're gonna need some help for the next part."

Hobie jumped to his feet. Amazing how anybody could do that after the day they'd both put in, but that was Hobie. "Right on it, Boss," he called softly as he dogtrotted off into the distance, going in the exact opposite direction from the posse.

"Son of a goddamn bitch!" Chambers snarled under his breath when he saw the Mexicans dragging off the body that had been hidden from him, until that moment, by weeds.

There went four hundred in gold, bumping and thudding over every jumping cholla and barrel cactus between here and the hacienda. A goddamn shame, that's what it was. No, a goddamn crime!

He sat on his rock, shaking with anger, until the posse had ridden out of sight. And then he trained his scope on the campfire and those gathered around it. He was going to take out somebody, by God, just to get himself even again.

But as he stared down toward the fire, he realized that he couldn't hit anything more of the man he thought was Hard to Kill than his boot. He shifted his sights to the big man, the one who'd handed over Diego Mondragon.

He followed the man for a few minutes, deciding if it was worth it or not, weighing the values of a good clean kill of anyone, anything, over the chances that he might not slip away so goddamn free this time. And at last, cursing under his breath, he lowered his rifle's muzzle.

The hell with it.

He'd ride back to the hacienda and see Montoya and get his money. It was going to fall quite a bit short of what it would have been, but he couldn't help that. At least he still had most of the cash money they'd taken off ol' Hard to Kill's horse before it had busted its leg.

That almost made up for it, but not quite.

"Not quite" would have to do.

Carefully, he began to make his way down the sharp incline.

Garner was aware they were in a bad place—out in the open, with scant cover, should they need it—but he still couldn't move Teach more than a few feet. Not until they built a travois, anyhow. And besides, the horses—at least, Fly and Faro—were all out. He would ask no more of them tonight.

Hobie had walked them cool, and while he went to fetch the women and the horse they'd stolen, Garner had curried and fed and watered them. He'd also seen to Diego Mondragon's Paso Fino.

He admired that horse. Pasos were flashy and fancy steppers, and from what he'd heard, a pleasure to ride. He'd never been on one, himself. He figured they were kind of like Plantation Walkers—stylish enough, and an easy horse for a man to ride when all he had to do was laze around a plantation all day, checking fields and such, or when he was showing off in a parade. But not much good for hard riding or roping or cutting, and therefore useless to him.

He patted the black stallion's neck. "But you're a handsome sonofabitch, aren't you, fella?" he asked the horse.

It answered with a bob of its head and a swing of its flowing ebony forelock.

He heard footsteps and the crunch of hooves lazily approaching, and turned to see Hobie and the women, leading the stolen chestnut, emerging from the darkness.

He signaled to Hobie to take care of the chestnut, then hiked back over to the fire.

"Black's got a bowed tendon," he said as he sat down. "He'll need several months of pasture rest."

Will, still sitting in the exact same place that Garner had left him, said, "Might's well shoot the poor thing, then. Doubt you'll find anybody in Arizona to take a fool horse like that."

Garner grunted. "Spoken like a true cavalryman."

The women joined them. The young one, Becky, came and sat down across the fire from him, while Mary Teach went directly to her husband's side. He knew Will had told her what had happened to Teach since that day she'd been taken, and her face was streaked with tears.

She wasn't crying anymore.

She was a strong woman, hiding her tears from her man when he was down, especially after all he figured she'd been through. Garner had a feeling that she'd been worth coming down the Mexico for, all right. And he also had a feeling that these two, Mary and Sam Teach, would stick together. He'd seen too many women, the victims of Indians or rampaging cowboys or *bandidos*, who, after living through that horror, had been sooner or later cast aside by their men.

Not Mary Teach, though, he thought, and not Sam. This was one marriage that was written in ink.

"Hobie!" he shouted.

A blond head stuck up over the chestnut's back and shouted back, "What?"

"Bring up something for supper when you get through," Garner called.

Garner thought he heard a little cussing, but paid it no mind. Frowning, he was staring into the distance, in the direction of their sniper's dull-silver former perch.

23

Milt Chambers jogged out of the pass, still cussing up a storm. Internally, at least. He was angry about having left ol' Hard to Kill once again, of course, but he was mostly angry about his bounty money.

If nothing else, he should have had the man's horse for his own. As it was, he led the strayed roan behind him. It limped along, trying to keep up. Maybe they'd pay something for its return.

He doubted it, though.

It was late, and the once-clear skies threatened to cover the moon with tattered, newly arrived clouds. He wondered if he should stop and camp for the night.

No, he decided. Unless it looked like the moon was going to go all the way under and settle the land into permanent dark, he'd keep going. Maybe they'd have some decent food at the hacienda. Either that, or he could find his way back into town again and eat at the cantina. A bed, even a tick-ridden bed, sounded a whole lot better than a rock-and-stone mattress, that was for certain.

But then, what if Smeed was there? That was all he

needed, on top of everything else that had gone wrong, for Smeed to turn up and demand his half of the sale money. By now, Chambers was thinking of it as his and his alone—minus, of course, his goddamn bounty money.

Thieves!

He began to make out what he thought was a rider in the distance. One of those flimsy clouds floated across the moon for a second, and he couldn't see. Maybe it had been a pronghorn or a stray steer. There were a few of those out here.

But then the cloud passed, and he saw it was a man, all right, and substantially nearer than he had been before.

He squinted, and recognized the black sombrero and the pattern on the serape. "Shit," he grumbled. It was Montoya.

What the hell. Might as well get it over with.

He hailed Montoya at right about the same moment as Montoya hailed him, and they rode toward each other at a walk.

"Ah, good evening, my friend!" said Montoya, once they were within speaking distance. "How goes the hunt?"

The thought that maybe Montoya hadn't sent those boys out looking for Diego Mondragon crossed Chambers's mind.

The two rode up even with each other, and reined in their horses. "All I found was this horse," Chambers said. "One'a yours, I reckon. Had Diego in my sights," he lied, "but a goddamn posse of your men rode off, draggin' him."

Montoya nodded, "I passed them on the way out. There was not much left of the body, I am afraid. I am very sorry you were robbed of your reward, Señor Chambers."

Well, it was something, anyhow. Wasn't nearly enough to make up for the loss of four hundred in gold, but he had to stay on this fellow's good side until he got his sale money.

After? That was another thing entirely.

He was already having pleasant thoughts about the things he'd do to Montoya. Things he would have liked to do to that posse, and more especially, that entire contingent back up north, huddled around their pathetic campfire.

"But I thought," Montoya continued, "that Diego was already dead when they found him."

The two reined their horses around, and started ambling south, toward the hacienda. The roan limped behind.

"That's true," said Chambers amiably. "But I had him in my sights when one'a them other fellers got him. One'a them American fellers what your boys picked Diego up from, I mean."

The moon faded, covered by tatters of clouds, and with it went Chambers's range of visibility. What had been bright silver a moment before was now shadowed in deep blues and blacks and purples.

Montoya grunted. Was he frowning? Chambers couldn't see, but he didn't think he liked it.

He was riding on Montoya's off side, and let his right hand slip slowly toward his holster. And all the time, he was thinking, *Benefit of the doubt, give him the benefit. He's got your money, remember?*

But that bad feeling he had wouldn't go away.

"I see," said Montoya. "At least you have found a horse. It is ours?"

"I reckon so," Chambers said creamily. "Sportin' the same brand as the nag you ride. There any reward for him?"

Montoya moved, but only to rest his wrist on the saddle's horn. "I suppose it could be arranged. Did you see anything else of interest while you were up there? The person attached to that horse, for example?"

"Saw a couple of them women you sold for us, if that's what you mean," Chambers said. The moon was still shrouded, and he still had his right hand on the butt of his gun. Montoya was grating on him. There was something he couldn't put his finger on, something about the man's attitude. Maybe it was just animal instinct, and Lord knows, Chambers had enough of that.

"Both of them?" Montoya asked.

"Yeah," Chambers said. "They was there for a while, but I didn't see 'em when your boys rode in. Fact is, I think one of the horses disappeared, too. Hope you didn't sell 'em to somebody with a mind to take 'em north of the border."

Montoya reined in his horse, and Chambers followed suit. His hand tightened almost imperceptibly on the grip of his gun.

"What?" Chambers asked.

Montoya seemed to be considering the answer. Or killing him. Maybe he wanted to keep the sale money for himself.

Chambers gently, slowly, began to ease his gun from its holster.

But then Montoya spoke. "Let the roan go, Señor. You and I have more important things to do before we ride south."

Montoya reined his horse around and started north again, which left Chambers just sitting there like some fool.

"Hey, where you goin'?" called Chambers as he jammed the gun back into its holster, then reluctantly pulled his rope from the lame roan's neck.

"I will explain on the way," Montoya shouted back. He was only twenty feet away, but he was already almost lost in the darkness.

Chambers reined his horse around, too, and shaking his head, followed.

An hour and a half later, they had stumbled their way through the darkness to the north end of the pass, and just managed to catch the occasional, tiny flicker from the campfire in the distance.

Montoya sat his horse, palms on the saddle horn, thinking. Chambers had told him there were four men and the two women who had escaped, and that one of the men, possibly two, were wounded.

Montoya hadn't told Chambers about the women's escape, hadn't hinted that he had no large payment to make to Chambers for them. He had just told Chambers that his marksmanship skills were needed, and that he would pay far more for the murder of these six than for Diego.

It had been enough for Chambers. And as for Montoya, he needed Chambers right now. Later, there would be time for the other.

Despite everything, Montoya's mouth twitched into a sort of smile. He would carry out one of the final wishes of his *patrón*, and he would carry it out in style.

Next to him, Chambers had that rifle to his shoulder, and he was grimly staring through the scope. Montoya waited.

"Ain't no way in hell I can hit 'em from here," Chambers finally said, and lowered the rifle. "Too damn dark."

"Then we will go closer, no?" Montoya said.

Chambers stuck the rifle's stock against his thigh. "I think we should wait," he said in a tone that most assuredly did not show the proper respect—for Montoya or anyone else.

"You will pardon me for asking," Montoya said creamily, "but why?"

"Moon's gotta slip free of them clouds sooner or later," Chambers said. He shook that grimy horsetail of his, which had been caught on his collar, free, then added, "I'll be better from a distance. Don't like close-in fightin' 'less the odds is a little more in my favor. You said two hundred apiece, right?"

"Correct."

Montoya figured that Chambers's best odds were when his target was an unarmed, helpless woman, but said nothing.

Only when Chambers turned to head back inside the mouth of the pass did Montoya speak. "No," he said. "We will leave the horses here and go closer on foot."

Chambers frowned. "Why? We got time. Hell, we can wait till mornin' if we have to."

Montoya drew himself up. "Because I want them now. You may leave if your wishes run contrary to mine."

Chambers appeared to mull it over. And at last, he said, "Fine. You just better not go steppin' on nothin' noisy, that's all."

It was as Montoya had thought. The call of money came first on Chambers's list of priorities. It did with most of these men who brought them the women. He smiled to himself as he dismounted, and pulled his rifle from its boot. "Very good," he said.

Once they took care of the people in the distance, he would kill Chambers, too. Then he would sling the body over a horse and take him back to the rancho, to be ground up like his partner. He was fairly sure that would have been Lopez's wish, and he would fulfill it.

But their horses, that was another matter. Now that Lopez was dead, he couldn't be certain what the future held for him. Señora Lopez would likely sell the *Patrón*'s holdings and move her household to Mexico City, to be near her married daughters. If that were to be the case, a nice string of horses would give him a good start on his new life.

But first things first.

Slowly, Montoya and Chambers crept forward through the clouded night, toward the tiny flicker in the distance.

"Got them settled back behind those rocks?" Garner whispered as Hobie crouched down beside him. Garner had his spyglass trained on the fire in the distance. His rifle was at his side.

"Yup," replied Hobie, also in a whisper. "Both of 'em. But Will's pretty mad that he can't do anything to help."

Garner half-smiled. "He would be," he replied softly. The horses were dozing on the picket line. He could just make out Faro's rump, the coppery color of his hide glistening bay-blue in the firelight. Shame to leave them down there. They'd had quite a hike up here, he and Hobie carefully carrying Teach between them, and the women propping up big Will Thurlow. Next to him, they both looked like children.

But it was the only way.

"All right," said Garner. "You know what to do."

"Right," murmured Hobie, and then yawned. It had been an awfully long day for both of them. "You got enough ammo?"

Garner patted the cartridge box beside him. "You got the spare spyglass?"

Hobie put a hand to one of his vest pockets. "You know, that feller might not even come back."

"Hope not," said Garner. His spyglass swept the darkness beyond the fire. He wished the moon would come back out. Hell, he wished he was home in his own bed. "Go on," he said. "And don't fall asleep."

"I'm goin'," grumbled Hobie, and scuttled off, disappearing into the night.

Garner had planned it out pretty well, he hoped. He'd sent Hobie off to the north, where there was a small rise that he could get up, and rocks he could get behind. It, like this place, was roughly seventy or eighty yards from the campfire. Once Hobie got into place, they'd be at almost a ninety-degree angle to each other.

Garner caught something in the distance. A glint. Could have been a coyote's eye, but it could have been something else, too. The glance of light off a rifle barrel or a concho. He didn't think he'd imagined it, although it was there for only a fraction of a second.

When a further search of the darkness produced nothing but black, he trained his glass back on the fire. There they were: six bedrolls, each containing a "body." They'd been hard-pressed to dig up enough to plump them out with, and Hobie's roll was filled out with a busted-up tumbleweed, the covering blanket held in place by rocks.

Garner comforted himself that the sniper, if and when he come back to finish the job, would probably aim and fire from a good distance out, then come in to check his handiwork. He'd told Hobie to wait until he could actually see the sonofabitch with his naked eye.

Then again, he might not come back at all.

And just when Garner almost had himself talked into thinking that they were going to have a quiet night after all, that the sniper who'd shot Will was miles south, he saw the rapid sparks of gunfire in the distance, like far-off, exploding fireflies. The first of the sound came to him after the third or fourth flash.

His rifle was at his shoulder by the time the last bedroll had jerked from the impact.

"Wait for it, Hobie," he muttered through clenched teeth as the last shot sounded. His eyes were trained on the direction from which the shots had come. "Just wait for it."

24

Hobie felt his stomach lurch to the side when the first gunshots went off. His finger tightened on the trigger, but he made himself hold on. He'd been through lots of tight situations with Garner. Tighter than this one, he reminded himself. But it still didn't help to drop his stomach back into place.

The wait for the shots to end seemed interminable, although he knew it was only a few seconds, if that. The fact that he knew it didn't help, either, and he cringed when his bedroll, packed with saddlebags and sage, jerked at the impact.

That coward!

Bad enough that he had to go and shoot Will from far off, but now he'd come back for the rest of them. Who the heck was that feller, anyway?

Hobie only realized that he'd broken out in a sweat when a bead rolled off the end of his nose and hit his hand. Still, he didn't move. He kept that rifle trained on the spot the flashes of gunpowder had come from.

And then the backshooting coward strolled into view.

• • •

Garner stiffened.

In the distance, the sniper slowly came into view, his rifle casually swinging at his side. He was a middle-sized man, lean, and when he turned slightly, Garner saw that he had a long horsetail that ended halfway down his back.

Garner had never seen him before.

But someone had.

From behind him, he heard one of the women gasp. He turned to tell her to be quiet, for Christ's sake, but she was already on her feet. Becky Lowell stood there, frozen, her finger pointing to the man at their fire, the man who had just murdered their bedrolls.

"It's him," she said in a strained whisper. "It's him, Mary."

And then she went down. Garner only realized as she fell that she'd been toppled at the knees by Mary Teach, who now had a hand firmly clamped over the girl's mouth.

He barely heard Mary's whisper of, "Shut up, you little fool!"

Garner looked back down toward the fire just in time to see the sniper raise his rifle again and scout the distance. The scope was headed their way, and he signaled Mary to get Becky back behind the rocks. They made it, just barely. When Garner dared look again, the scope had passed them, and the sniper was looking south.

Just then a second man—big, muscular, and Mexican—came into view. He said something to the sniper, although Garner couldn't make out the words, and the sniper lowered his weapon. The Mexican's gun was drawn, and he gestured with it at the motionless bedrolls.

The sniper laughed and raised his rifle again. This time, he fired point-blank at each bedroll. But before he shot the last of them, his bullet lifted the blanket off one, exposing the broken brush beneath.

He didn't see, but the second man, the Mexican, did. He darted back toward the horses.

Garner fired, but missed. "Sonofabitch," he muttered, and trained his rifle on the sniper.

But the sniper had seen the flash of his shot, and was already taking aim.

Garner ducked down behind the boulders fast, but still got a forehead full of granite shards when the sniper's bullet hit the boulder sheer inches from his face.

Hobie didn't miss, though. Garner saw the rifle's smoky discharge and heard its report just an instant after the sniper fired. And when he peered up over the rock again, mopping blood from his forehead, the sniper was sprawled on his back beside the fire. Dead, by the looks of it. At least, he wasn't complaining about the hand that was in the flames.

Garner's attention went back to the man hiding between their horses. "Should've built a second fire over there," he grumbled when all he could make out was a murky sea of dark trunks and shadows where the horses' legs were supposed to be. The Mexican could be crouched down anywhere in their midst.

It never occurred to Garner to just start shooting horses.

Wiping his brow of blood again, he signaled to Hobie to stay put and draw the Mexican's fire. Hobie began to shoot over the horses' heads, and Garner dashed out from behind the cover of boulders, raced to the next cluster of rocks, dived, and rolled behind them.

By the time he reached this temporary safety, his eyes were full of blood again. He cursed and mopped his forehead once more, grinding his teeth against the pain when it brought out several of those granite chips from beneath his skin.

But this wasn't anything compared to what Will had suffered, or especially what Teach was going through, or those women. The wound stung like hell, but it was mostly annoying. Quickly, he pulled his hat forward until it rested on top of his eyebrows. He figured he'd end up with a hat full of blood, but at least it would keep his vision clear while he needed it.

He was closer to the horses now, but he still couldn't see anything. He glanced overhead, hoping to find that the moon was just about free of clouds. But it wasn't so. The clouds were rolling in more thickly, if that were possible.

"Come on out, mister!" he heard Hobie call. "You ain't got no hope of gettin' out of here in one piece if you don't."

The only reply was a gunshot, issuing from the horses' midst.

Over on the picket line, Faro swung in Garner's direction and half-reared. The black Paso Fino beside him snorted and skittered the opposite way.

"You just gave yourself away, friend," Garner muttered.

Even while the horses were still shying, Hobie returned fire. Garner immediately took off around the far end of the boulders and ran, in a crouch, directly toward the horses.

The Mexican was busy firing back at Hobie when Garner cut around the far end of the picket line, panting hard.

Nonetheless, in two long strides he had the Mexican under the point of a gun. But the Mexican had his back to him, and was cursing, reloading his pistol.

"Hold it," said Garner.

The Mexican froze.

"Drop that smoke-wagon," Garner said.

The Mexican dropped his gun. It landed in the dust and the Paso Fino, still spooked, promptly stepped on it.

"Stand up."

Slowly, the man stood.

Garner sighed. "Turn around."

The Mexican began to turn, and it wasn't until he was sideways to Garner that Garner caught the glint of something in his hand.

Garner jumped back just as the Mexican wheeled and lashed out. He missed being sliced open like a fish being gutted, but he stumbled and went down.

The Mexican was on him before Garner could bring up his gun, and the shot he did manage to get off went wild. He heard a horse scream, but he didn't have time to do anything about it. The Mexican's knife was at his throat, nipping, biting at the skin, and the only thing holding it back from deeper, more tender flesh was the strength of Garner's left arm.

It was fading fast, though, and his hat had gone somewhere, knocked off in the fall. Blood streamed down his forehead and into his eyes as he tried to bring his gun to bear. But the Mexican had as tight a grip on his gun-hand wrist as *he* did on the Mexican's knife hand, and grunting, the Mexican whispered, "This is what they call a Mexican standoff, is it not?"

Garner brought his knee up hard, square into the Mexican's crotch. Immediately, the Mexican weakened—but only a little—and Garner was able to bring the gun between them. He still couldn't shake loose the man's knife hand, and he was fading fast.

"Quit it!" he growled through clenched teeth. "Settle down or I'll shoot," he added, even though he knew damn well that the gun's barrel was aimed square at the man's side. The worst a bullet could do at that angle was rip through some body fat and maybe a little meat. But it was the only shot he figured he'd be able to get off.

The Mexican said, "Go ahead. Pull the trigger. I will still cut your throat, Señor. After that kick, it would be my pleasure." And then he smiled.

"You'll never make it two yards," Garner grunted.

Blood coursing from his forehead had blinded him by this time, and the last thing he'd seen halfway clearly was the Mexican's grin. "My man's got you covered," he lied.

The Mexican quickly craned his head around, and Garner took advantage of the situation to twist with all his might. He managed to roll the surprised Mexican off him, but his strength gave out halfway through.

The Mexican's knife hand had lowered, and the jab he made with it took Garner just beneath the collarbone. Pain spiraled through him, but he ignored it. He pulled the trigger, and when he felt the Mexican sag, he hastily wiped his eyes.

The Mexican's smile, the last thing he remembered seeing, had turned to a look of surprise, then disbelief. He stared into Garner's eyes, then looked down at the blood-stain spreading rapidly over his chest. He opened his mouth, as if to ask a question, but he never spoke. He just went limp.

Garner felt his neck for a pulse. There was none.

"Nice work, Boss."

Startled, Garner looked up. Hobie stood a yard from Garner's feet. One hand was on Faro's flank. The other was just lowering the gun in it.

Garner sat up, grimacing. "Where the hell'd you come from?"

Hobie frowned, and bent to him. "Thought you seen me! Heard you tell him so."

"I didn't see you. That was just a— Ouch!"

Hobie pulled the knife free. "You ain't stuck too bad, Boss," he said thoughtfully. "Take a couple'a stitches, maybe. How's your head? Looks terrible."

"You mean to tell me you were standing there the whole time?" Garner demanded angrily.

When Hobie didn't answer him, he asked, "Well, why the hell didn't you shoot?"

Hobie shrugged. "I was afraid, since I was so close,

that the slug would go right through him and into you. Like that deal when we picked up Grayson Klum last spring. Remember?"

Garner remembered, all right. Somehow, he always ended up wrestling with these fellows. And Hobie'd shot clean through Grayson Klum and on into Garner's forearm. He was lucky his arm had been in the way, or else it would have gone into his gut.

"Yeah," Garner said. "I recall." Hobie reached down, and Garner wasn't too proud to accept a hand up. Besides, he didn't figure that he could have stood up on his own. He shook off Hobie's hand and looked around to see Mary Teach and Becky Lowell just coming out from behind the boulders. Then he looked up. The last tatters of clouds were slipping on past, and the moon was coming out again. A little late, he thought.

"I heard a horse earlier," he said.

Hobie' s voice brought his gaze back down to earth. "You scarred this Paso, that's for certain," he said, indicating a long bullet mark on the black's rump. "But he's not gonna croak. I'll put some salve on it. As if I haven't had enough to do today."

Garner half-smiled at that, and took three steps toward the fire before he keeled over.

Six weeks later

Hobie rode back from town and into the barnyard at about three in the afternoon. But instead of going straight to the barn, he rode up to the house and tied Fly to the rail. He climbed the steps to the porch, announced, "Got a letter for you, Boss," and slapped it down on the little table beside Garner's chair.

Garner looked down at it, then back up at Hobie. "You're not going to put your horse away?"

"In a minute," Hobie` said, and sat down in the other

chair. "Well?" he asked, thumbing back his hat. "You gonna sit there all day, or are you gonna open it?"

Without looking at it, Garner picked it up. "What is it this time? If Holling Eberhart is trying to get me out in the field again, or changed his mind about not pressing charges against you, I'm going to tell him to—"

He glanced at the envelope, then squinted. "From the Teaches?" he asked.

Hobie nodded. "C'mon, hurry up and read it. I want to hear how that fancy surgeon made out. And U.S. Marshal Eberhart knows Ned Smallie is an idiot. He ain't gonna press charges."

"You weren't so sure of yourself a month back, when we went up to see him," Garner muttered, and patted his pocket for his reading glasses.

After he pulled them out and put them on, he tore a corner of the envelope, them slitted it open with his forefinger. He took out a single sheet of paper, covered in neat handwriting on both sides.

"Read it!" demanded Hobie.

"I swear," Garner growled, "you're like a kid wanting candy!"

Hobie didn't say anything this time.

Garner began to read aloud.

" *'Dear Marshal Garner and Marshal Hobson,'* " he began. " *'We have just returned from Denver, and I must happily report to you that Sam's operation was a great success. Dr. Jarvis said that had the bullet been only an eighth of an inch to the right, Sam would have been paralyzed forever. As it is, he is walking with crutches and ultimately will be back to his old self. It's all I can do to hold him down.'* "

He continued. " *'Sam says that he has decided to forgive you for not picking up laudanum in Mexico, since you gave us that Paso Fino. He's a good horse.'* " When he looked up at Hobie, he was grinning. "That sonofabitch!" he said, shaking his head. "Sometimes it just doesn't pay to go around saving people's lives. Forgive me, my ass!"

Hobie smiled, too, then leaned across the table. "What else does she say?"

Garner paused to turn the paper over, and said, "She goes on, *I am not having nightmares so often, and Sam is wonderful. Will is mended good as new, and Bess is surely happy to have him back. She sends her regards and says if you ever get down this way, she'll bake you a pie. Becky is fine, too. Bess appreciates the help. Will has straightened out the business about Becky's ranch, and he is holding it in trust for her until she is eighteen. Will and Bess were grand to take her in. The poor girl had no one. Come see us sometime! Five months from now, we expect a blessed event. Regards, Mary Teach.'*"

Hobie, looking worried, started counting on his fingers, and Garner said, "She was in a family way before. Will told me."

Hobie's hands went flat on the table. "No wonder Teach was so set on getting her back," he said thoughtfully. Then he grumbled, "Aw, nobody tells me anything! And she doesn't say how she and Teach are gettin' on."

Garner dug into the envelope again and pulled out a piece of stiff cardboard. He looked at it and smiled. He handed it across the table to Hobie.

Sam and Mary Teach had posed for a recent photograph—while they were up in Denver, by the imprint on the back of the cardboard—and they looked as happy and as in love as any newlyweds.

"Oh, I think they're all right," Garner said as he tucked his glasses away. "I think they're going to do just fine. Now, go put up Fly."

WOLF MACKENNA

THE BURNING TRAIL
0-425-18694-6
"COMPELLING WESTERN WITH FAST ACTION
AND ENGAGING CHARACTERS."
—PETER BRANDVOLD

DUST RIDERS
0-425-17698-3
A VENGEFUL COWBOY AND A TENDERFOOT YANKEE
JOIN FORCES TO TRACK MURDEROUS THIEVES
THROUGH TERRAIN THAT'S EQUALLY DEADLY.

GUNNING FOR REGRET
0-425-17880-3
SHERIFF DIX GRANGER AND HIS PRISONER FIND
THEMSELVES IN THE TOWN OF REGRET, WAITING OUT A
STORM. WHEN ONE OF THE TOWN'S RESIDENTS
KILLS AN APACHE, DIX KNOWS IT'S UP TO HIM TO
DEFEND THE TOWN FROM APACHE VENGEANCE.

Penguin Group (USA) Inc.
Online

Your Internet gateway to a virtual environment with
hundreds of entertaining and enlightening books
from Penguin Group (USA) Inc.

*While you're there, get the latest buzz on
the best authors and books around—*

Tom Clancy, Patricia Cornwell, W.E.B. Griffin,
Nora Roberts, William Gibson, Robin Cook,
Brian Jacques, Catherine Coulter, Stephen King,
Ken Follett, Terry McMillan, and many more!

**Penguin Group (USA) Inc. Online is located at
http://www.penguin.com**

PENGUIN GROUP (USA) Inc.
NEWS

Every month you'll get an inside look at our upcom-
ing books and new features on our site. This is an
ongoing effort to provide you with the most
up-to-date information about
our books and authors.

**Subscribe to Penguin Group (USA) Inc. News at
http://www.penguin.com/newsletters**